*ar

★ "A side-
spotlight c
American
The Perks
results." —

"Take one
gay best fr
headings a
understanc
genuine de

"Witty. . .
John Gree

"Disarmin
interior mi
the world."

"Perceptiv
a playfully
English cla
classics." —

two parties, one tux*

one tux*

*and a very short film about *the grapes of wrath*

STEVEN GOLDMAN

BLOOMSBURY

NEW YORK BERLIN LONDON

Quotes on pages 36–39 from *The Grapes of Wrath* by John Steinbeck published by
Penguin Great Books of the 20th Century

Quote on page 135 from *Ghostbusters II*

Published by Bloomsbury U.S.A. Children's Books
175 Fifth Avenue, New York, New York 10010

The Library of Congress has cataloged the hardcover edition as follows:
Goldman, Steven.
Two parties, one tux, and a very short film about the Grapes of Wrath /
by Steven Goldman.—1st U.S. ed.
p.   cm.
Summary: Mitch, a shy and awkward high school junior, negotiates the difficult social
situations he encounters, both with girls and with his best friend David, after David
reveals to him that he is gay.
ISBN-13: 978-1-59990-271-5 • ISBN-10: 1-59990-271-0 (hardcover)
[1. Friendship—Fiction. 2. Interpersonal relations—Fiction. 3. Dating (Social
customs)—Fiction. 4. Homosexuality—Fiction. 5. High schools—Fiction.
6. Schools—Fiction.] I. Title.
PZ7.G56924Tw2008   [Fic]—dc22   2008011587

ISBN-13: 978-1-59990-393-4 • ISBN-10: 1-59990-393-8 (paperback)

Typeset by Westchester Book Composition
Printed in the U.S.A. by Quebecor World Fairfield
1 3 5 7 9 10 8 6 4 2

All papers used by Bloomsbury U.S.A. are natural, recyclable products
made from wood grown in well-managed forests. The manufacturing processes
conform to the environmental regulations of the country of origin.

For Kat and my boys,
and although he and I aren't in this book,
Bert too

two parties, one tux*

*and a very short film about *the grapes of wrath*

CHAPTER 1

Party (a, to, of)

We are . . .

We are standing at a party, a still, quiet eddy in the swirl of motion and noise. David is holding a can of Diet Coke as if it could be a beer, but his facial expression and confident stance make it clear that he wants it to be a Diet Coke, and who are you to question that. I am holding a beer, sort of wishing it were a Diet Coke. We aren't talking, but not because we aren't talking. We aren't talking because this is what we do at parties. We stand here. "Here" is always somewhere near the midsection of the party animal. Not on the fringes (basement playroom, upstairs bedrooms, backyard), because that's where everything happens (drugs, sex, fights). We aren't really up for any of that kind of stuff and no one really wants us there anyway. Not near the front door either; that would invite too much scrutiny, imply some sort of eagerness. Front-door people want to be seen.

We don't want to appear to want to be here. Everything we do implies that we might not need to be here long at all. Any moment now, we could head out because there is something better happening somewhere else. There isn't, but we would like to give that impression. We stand in the den off to one side with our backs near the wall, holding our Diet Coke and our beer, nodding every once in a while at people going by, but not really talking to them any more than we are talking to each other.

"What are we doing here?" I ask David, after about an hour of this.

"Mitchell," David answers after a sufficiently long pause to show that he's in no hurry to answer the question, "we are partying."

I nod.

We may be here to party, but I am here because David gave me a ride. David always gives me rides. That's how we talk about it. He called me this afternoon and said, "I think I'm going to this party, need a ride?" I said yes. Listening to us talk, you would guess that our lives are mostly about transportation.

David gave me a ride because we are friends. We are friends because we have been sitting together at lunch since day one of junior year. We sit together at lunch because we are the only two juniors who signed up for an otherwise freshman-filled art course and therefore we are the only two juniors who have early lunch. Following this logic, I realize that I am standing at this party because I chose to take ancient history rather than art in ninth grade. The sheer randomness impresses me.

From my post by the wall, I watch Danielle sit in a chair. She is dressed in jeans and a sweater, her hair is pulled back and her lips are shiny. A purposeful, very put-together casualness. Her legs are crossed at the knees and she is leaning just slightly forward, intent but not committed to the conversation. She's smiling the kind of perfect smile that has to be fake because it looks too natural. Ryan, all six feet and change of him, stands in front of her, animation to her stillness. He's not dancing, but it is a dance: the way he moves his hands, tilts his head, slowly works her smile into a giggle and then a laugh. They are completely by themselves in a room full of people.

"Couldn't you just puke?" Mariel says. I hadn't realized that she was beside me or that it was so obvious that I was staring at Danielle and Ryan. "True love and all that crap. David."

"Mariel," David answers with a very slight nod.

"You should be pacing yourself," Mariel says. "You know what they say about drinking carbonated beverages and driving."

"Mitchell's got my back. He's just drinking beer."

Mariel takes a pull from her bottle of water. I may be holding a beer, but we are the lightweight corner. We stand quietly for a few minutes.

"I was telling Mitchell here that he should go out for

wrestling next year," David says as if that conversation hadn't taken place at lunch.

Mariel makes a face.

"What's wrong with wrestling?" he asks.

"Nothing, as long as you're naked and in love." She gives me a quick scan top to bottom. Mariel is a fellow nerd. If she weren't, her light brown skin, long black curls, and high cheekbones might make her intimidating. "Field hockey," she says after thinking for a moment.

"It's a girl's sport," I point out.

"Trevor plays it."

"They make him wear a skirt."

"Which he looks great in. He also rides to games on a bus with twenty-four girls who think he's cool. Beats wrestling."

"You can't play field hockey," David tells me earnestly after Mariel moves on. "Trevor is the only person in the school who can possibly get away with playing field hockey, because he's six-two, has an Australian accent, and every female in the school is dying to jump on his stick."

I'm five-seven, no accent, and there's no line of excited females wanting to jump on any of my sports equipment. I'm not Trevor. I assure David that I'm not planning on going out for field hockey.

We aren't . . .

Two hours later, I follow David to his car. He wonders out loud whether it will be expensive to replace the hedges that someone drove through. I have no opinion on hedge prices.

David drives me home. My sister is also being dropped off. We sit in the car while she makes out with some guy on our front porch. Neither of us can tell who the guy is from the back. She has to know we are sitting here, but she has chosen to ignore us. Carrie doesn't embarrass easily. It makes me uncomfortable to watch my little sister kiss whoever it is she's kissing, although David notes that he is nicely dressed and they are really only kissing, not doing much touching. He guesses that she isn't convinced about this guy. They finish kissing and Carrie goes inside followed by our dog, which was also watching. The male, who we can now identify as Peter, is in our class, which makes him only a grade ahead of Carrie. For her, that's slumming. He smiles as he walks past us, like maybe he just won something. Neither of us are convinced that he has a rat's chance in a trash compactor of ever kissing her again, but I'm guessing he doesn't know that yet. Peter isn't the kind of guy who'll stop and talk to us—not in the hallway at school, not at a party, and certainly not after playing mash-mouth with my sister on our front porch. He pretends he doesn't see us. We stare at him, in the hopes of making him feel a little self-conscious. Hard to tell if it works.

David and I don't play mash-mouth. We aren't a couple. We're just two guys coming home from a party.

CHAPTER 2

Two Guys

David is gay

David is gay. He told me at lunch.

I think I said something like, "I'm sure they think we're gay," about the freshmen who see us always eating lunch together, and he said, "Mitchell, I *am* gay," and I laughed because I was sure he was joking. It didn't sound like a joke, but David never sounds like he's joking.

"I don't think you're gay," I said confidently, as if I was reassuring him he wasn't dying of some horrifying multi-syllabic disease.

"I'm serious."

"You're gay."

"Yes."

"Does everybody know this except me?"

"No."

"Does anyone know this besides me?"

"No. Just you."

And you tell me at lunch? He picks up his apple and holds it in his hand like maybe he's forgotten what to do with it. His mouth is set with his usual confidence, but his eyes, behind his glasses, don't seem as sure. He's testing the waters, waiting for my reaction. Usually I get the feeling that he doesn't care about what I think, but this is different.

"I'm not," I say, trying not to sound defensive.

"I know."

"How do you know?"

"I just know. I can tell."

"No, you can't. I couldn't tell about you."

"Well, I can."

"Because you're gay?"

"Maybe."

"Well, maybe I could be gay."

"You're not."

"I'm not. Are you sure you are?" Maybe there was time to change his mind.

David rolls his eyes.

I start to ask why he's telling me, but he's telling me because I'm his best friend. He doesn't look any different to me than he did yesterday, but I guess he was gay then too, so I'm not sure why he should look any different. If anything, he looks more like himself than usual. Only David would make a confession like this at lunch.

"How long have you known?"

"I think I've always known."

"How come you've never told anyone?"

"Would you have?"

Maybe, but this is not the way I would have chosen to break the news. "Are you going to tell anyone?" I ask. "I mean, besides me."

"Do you tell anyone you're straight?"

No, I don't. Should I be telling people I'm straight? Is it wrong to assume that they should assume I am? I try to look like I'm taking all of this in stride. It is the reaction I think David wants. I take a bite of my sandwich and wonder what I'm supposed to say next. I don't ask him if he has done anything with a guy because I'm not sure I want to know. I'm much happier assuming David's homosexuality is simply hypothetical—much like my heterosexuality. I am convinced I'm straight, but it remains largely untested.

"Is there some reason you're bringing this up now?" I ask.

"You brought it up."

Did I? We're three-quarters of the way through our junior year of high school. For the last eight months, we've sat at this same table for lunch. We've seen on average a movie a week, hung out at each other's houses, gone to maybe seven parties together, and once drove to Thomasville to see the giant chair that sits on Main Street. Had I not noticed my best friend was gay all of that time? It just never came up?

I can't think of anything else to say about the topic. David finishes his apple. He can't think of anything else either.

"So now you know," he says.

So, now I know, but I don't know what I should do now that I know.

And I have my own issues

Sometimes a man got to do what he got to do. At seventeen, your mother can no longer choose your deodorant for you. I make my stand in the personal care aisle at Walgreens, ready to decide what kind of male I really am. There are so many choices. There are at least twenty-five different brands of deodorant at Walgreens. Even after eliminating the ones that are clearly marketed to women, there are still too many to choose from. I am paralyzed staring at the gels, powders, roll-ons, and sprays. I have spent more time standing here today than I have on my calculus homework.

I make the bold decision to go for direct application over spray. That eliminates some but brings me no closer to self-definition. I can't use something called "Eau de Toilette," even if it is made by a shoe company. I can't buy anything that sounds like my dad might use it, or anything sailor-like—way too hokey. And "powder fresh" doesn't sound like what I want people to think when they smell me. So I'm down to innocuous ones with names that imply dryness and protection, but even these are divided into mind-boggling subcategories. Cool Fusion? Energy Ultra? Wild Rain? Are these things I want in my armpits?

I take a deep breath and choose a high-endurance gel that sounds masculine and yet hygienic, with a promise of effectiveness. I then put it back on the shelf and instead take the same spray that my mother bought me last time, but I only buy the smallest possible size in case I change my mind when I get home. I don't want to be stuck with months of the wrong deodorant. I'm too embarrassed to have this be my only purchase, so I also buy two candy bars and a poker deck, even though I have never played poker. I do not look the cashier in the eye as she scans my purchases.

CHAPTER 3

Dark, Slightly Smelly Places in My Soul (and Elsewhere)

The Mushroom Club

Deep in the basement, in the very bowels of Richard White Day School, at the end of a long hall that runs behind the cafeteria, is a plain brown door. On the wall beside this door is a small brass plaque that seems out of place on the mustard-colored plaster. It reads:

FILM LAB

EQUIPMENT PROVIDED BY AN ANONYMOUS DONOR

1994

This is the fiefdom of Sydney Wallman, AV maven, film club sponsor, and the oldest true geek I've ever met. If he has ever set foot outside this room, I've never seen it. His desk, piled high with papers, DVDs, partially disassembled computers, and random pieces of electrical equipment, sits in the middle of the enormous space surrounded by an actual working television studio with separate workspaces for film or audio projects. It is an impressive amount of stuff and would probably be the kind of thing that would attract students if Wallman himself weren't so completely frightening. He has a small following of very dedicated trolls who spend most of their time immersed in role-playing games among the squalor of the film lab (Wallman sponsors several versions of geek clubs), but almost no one else ever ventures this far down the hall. Except, starting last semester, David and me.

We had to fulfill the art requirement somehow. Neither of us can draw or wanted to paint. We got closed out of photography and couldn't imagine doing pottery. I think the course we signed up for was called digital animation, but Wallman was not sufficiently impressed with David's or my computer skills, so he laughingly, or I guess cacklingly, suggested we use the stop-motion camera and do a Claymation project. Maybe he was joking. We said sure and he seemed intrigued by our agreement. The next day he provided us with Plasticine (which is like shiny clay), odd materials for sets, a caliper, and a documentary on some English guy we had never heard of. We then spent two weeks watching all of the Wallace and Gromit movies, *Chicken Run*, and episodes of an old demented children's show called *Pee-wee's Playhouse*. This soon became our favorite class.

"What kind of movie should we make?" David asked Wallman after we had finished watching everything Nick Park had ever made.

"Don't much care," Wallman said, chewing on his beard. "But it should have lots of blood. I usually recommend sex and violence, but sex with little clay figures is just sick, so I'd stick to violence. You guys are probably too young, but did you ever see any Mr. Bill?"

We spent most of the next week watching vintage *Saturday Night Live* clips. The true geeks, sitting hunched over their computer monitors translating pixels, began to resent us.

Our first film was a two-and-a-half-minute feature that David titled "Everything Wrong with the World." It consisted mostly of a giant dog peeing on various historical figures: Abraham Lincoln, Mahatma Gandhi, Julius Caesar. Wallman made us do storyboards for every scene and repetition turned out to be the easiest way to get to actual shooting. Thank God for Xerox machines. I think we had a vague idea that we were making some kind of good-versus-evil statement, but mostly we discovered that making anything recognizable out of Plasticine was tricky and Lincoln was about as good as we could do. For some reason, we also found the Bill-Gates-melting-in-dog-pee bit way too funny.

And then somehow we found ourselves signing up for Digital Animation 2, rather than Foundations of Economic

Theory, which was the elective we had been told to take by our academic advisors. We weren't Wallmanites, but we were willing to tolerate another semester of lunch with freshmen and sophomores for a chance to make another film.

◉ ◉ ◉

"I don't get it," Mariel says when she searches us out one study hall. The trolls stare at her as she walks through the gloom toward the back of the lab where all of our Claymation stuff is set up. The lab is lit mostly by glowing computer screens. The overhead fluorescent lights give Wallman a headache, and the few scattered lamps don't do much in a room with zero natural light. Maybe Wallman is a vampire. Mariel avoids touching anything she passes, as if she's concerned that something might pop out and bite her. Given the number of times females enter the film lab, she might actually have something to fear from the trolls. She watches us set up the scenery and place our favorite little Plasticine guy in the center of a giant table surrounded by four floor lamps. "What is so fascinating about filming squashed clay?"

It's hard to explain. The process is unbelievably slow. First you have to plan the whole scene, frame by frame. You then have to build sets and the actual characters. We spent four days trying to get our figures to stand up before Wallman explained what an armature was. It turns out that clay men need a little frame or they fall over. When you finally get to the actual filming, you set up the scene, position the clay figures, set the camera, take a shot, reposition the figures in the tiniest, most subtle of steps, and repeat. You have to have some time to spend. It isn't really a spectator sport.

"Exercising your OCD?" Mariel asks.

"More like playing with dolls in extreme slow motion," David says, using the caliper to measure the position of the figure's left hand. We are working on a wave.

Mariel looks around the lab. "Where did all this equipment come from?"

"Someone donated it," David explains, motioning for me to take the shot. "An anonymous donor. The prevailing theory is that Wallman bought it all himself with the money he saved by not having a house and sleeping in his office. There's some pretty cool stuff down here."

"Can I try?"

I look at David. He shrugs and shows Mariel how to manipulate the little figure. We get most of the wave done.

Wallman wanders over, eating a sandwich. "You should be using a green screen behind that," he says, then wanders away again.

"Do you know what a green screen is?" I ask David. I don't know why I ask. I can tell he has no idea from the look on his face.

"Does this mean we have to do all of that over again?" Mariel sounds stricken. We've been down here for the better part of a forty-minute period.

"Only if we want him to wave," David says, rubbing his nose with the palm of his hand. "So, Mariel, what are you doing tomorrow in study hall?"

Fourteen screens, each with its own sticky floor

The only actual homework for any of Wallman's courses is that you have to go see movies. Wallman shows some himself using a digital projector and a portable screen. His choices tend to be obscure or disgusting, sometimes both obscure and disgusting. Afterward he leads a discussion of the film's technical qualities. Content is irrelevant to Wallman. Sometimes he requires us to attend specific films in actual theaters. Last semester he sent David and me to watch an animation festival that was showing only at an arts theater in Charlotte. It was a two-hour drive each way on a school night, but it was worth it. Some weeks he just tells us to go see a movie.

"Movie?" David asks. It's a Thursday, but it does count as homework.

"Yeah," I answer.

"7:23?" he asks.

"Great," I answer.

But here's the deal. It is 7:15. I am waiting to be picked up by my friend David. What makes this not a date?

Okay. For starters, he's not paying. But would he pay

even if it was a date? Do people take each other to the movies? It sounds like something my parents would have done when they dated. My mother has this story she always tells about my dad being really late for their first date and how she sat, all dressed and made up, waiting for him. They never made it to the movie. Wait, what did they do if they didn't make it to the movie? Is that a story about my parents having sex? Why does my mother tell this story? Am I the girl here, waiting for David to come pick me up? No. Things are different, and this isn't a date.

Two. David and I have been going out for months. Going out to movies and parties and things, not *going out*. But if he was always gay, is it possible that we were *going out* going out and I didn't know about it? Can someone be accidentally dating?

Three. No kissing. No sex. No touching at all. Can't be a date, can it?

David picks me up. We go to see the movie and sit side by side in the nearly empty theater. I eat popcorn and stay well within the limits of my seat space. David doesn't seem any different. On the way home we talk a little about what we want to do with our film. We're just friends seeing a movie. What is wrong with me?

My bedroom

When I get home, waiting for me on the floor of my bedroom on a pile of fetid escapees from the laundry hamper is a small paperback book. It looks gray and cold, almost lonely. The cover is a black-and-white photograph of a guy in overalls with his mouth slightly open, his hair standing up in the wind. He does not look happy. A white box bisected by a thin black line sits two-thirds of the way down the page and contains only six words written in some odd, asymmetrical type. Above the line: John Steinbeck. Below the line: *The Grapes of Wrath*. There is nothing on the cover of this book that makes me want to open it.

I do not pick up the book. I do not want to read this book. I feel a surge of anger at having been asked to read this book. Isn't wrath a kind of anger? Do I have to read the book? I have to write a paper on this book, but does that mean I actually have to read it first?

I call David. He can't have been home for long. Does David wear pajamas?

"I don't want to read *The Grapes of Wrath*," I tell him.

"That would make writing the paper harder." He is being so unnecessarily rational. After all, I took really good notes in class; surely I could just fake this one through. Maybe my notes weren't that good, but I took notes; that has to be enough. Okay, my notes suck, but I wrote down words in my notebook and mostly listened. How much do I need to know to write this paper? I'm pretty sure I remember most of the characters' names.

"Come on," I say confidently, "how hard can it be to fake a paper?" He wouldn't know. Neither would I. We're the good kids. We work hard at school. We sit up in class and take notes. We read the syllabus and study for tests. What is wrong with us?

CHAPTER 4

Monday

School

There are six conversations. It helps to memorize the proper responses.

Most frequent:

"How did you do on the (test, paper, project, lab report, SATs)?"

"Okay, I guess." (Vague, never say, "Really good!")

Regular:

"You got an extra (pen, pencil, piece of paper, copy of your math homework)?"

No verbal response required. Nod and hand over. If the request is for a cigarette, smile weakly and shake your head.

The same people, every day:

"Hi."

"Hi."

Rare, more from adults:

"How's it going?"

"It's going." (Usually follow with a shrug to show that it *is*, but not too well.)

If standing with a group:

"Did you see (some movie, TV show, concert, Ryan and Danielle making out in the hall)?"

No response required if answer is no. Answer is always no if the question concerns Ryan and Danielle. If answer is yes, then a short, noncommittal "yeah" until the group preference is established, and then agree. Usually things suck.

If standing with a group of males discussing females:

"Did she . . . will she . . . did you see her . . . she's such a . . ."

There are no safe responses, since all imply some level of expertise. Stand quietly, exit ASAP.

School

I don't react much to chemistry as a rule. Labs are a game of trying to figure out what was supposed to happen, guessing the proper conclusion, and trying to finagle the data to support the right answer. I believe this is what is known as the scientific method. Mariel, my frequent lab partner and the will-be valedictorian of our class, has declared me a hazard and won't let me touch anything combustible or corrosive. Mostly I take dictation while she does the experiment. Lecture days are always a relief. Today's is on molecules randomly bouncing off each other. I spend the period mesmerized by how much of Simone's bra I can see through the persistent gap between the second and third buttons of her shirt. It is less than an inch of nondescript white—none of her actual breast is visible—but it is much more fascinating than anything I am being told about the chaos in a glass of water.

School

Mariel and David are laughing about something in front of Thad's locker. In all likelihood, it's Thad. A couple of lacrosse players walk down the hall followed by three cheerleaders—or if they aren't actually cheerleaders, they look like they would want to wear short skirts and stand on one another's shoulders to get a rise from the crowd. They exist in a separate high-school universe and they pass the rest of us as if they can't see us. Maybe they can't.

There are signs reminding us to register for the SATs. There's a bulletin board that displays last month's calendar surrounded by a lot of notices for events that happened long ago. But it's almost April. In September, everything is hung nicely. In October and November, someone dutifully replaces the old notices with new ones. By now, everyone has given up.

"Are you okay?" Carrie asks me when she passes me after B period. I must look upset, because she usually doesn't talk to me at school.

"Maybe," I answer, but I don't elaborate. She accepts my one-word response and lets the pull of the between-classes crowd drag her away.

School

There is a rhythm to the day. We don't march, we don't dance, but the movement of our feet isn't simple Brownian motion. Some genius has decreed that our schedule should rotate, but it's more of a lurch and tug. No one two three four five six seven. A and B start our day, then some combination of ones to fours except on Tuesdays and Thursdays, which have an activity period, and Wednesdays, which include time for a morning assembly, assuming we aren't on a shortened flex schedule. If it's Monday there's no fourth period, Tuesday no first. There's a logic without sense.

But we get there, mostly on time anyway. We have longer blocks for labs and seminars around tables and a gym with a real climbing wall, but it's still just school.

School

"Are you really going to eat that?" David asks, unwrapping his sandwich. David has one of three possible lunches.

To be more precise, David has one of three possible lunchmeats; the rest of the menu doesn't change at all. One apple, red; one small bag of chips, greasy; a piece of paper towel as a napkin; and a sandwich, white bread, mustard, meat. I haven't noticed a pattern to the meat itself but he only seems to eat roast beef, turkey, or ham sliced thinly. No cheese.

David does not seem to have a sense of humor about his lunch. I often try to convince him that there is some deep-seated pathology in his rigidly limited sandwich selection. But my efforts usually fail because I am always trying to convince him to trade lunches, and I have the world's worst lunches. My lunches consist of whatever happens to be in the fridge when we wake up in the morning. Cold lasagna. Pickles and cream cheese. Meatloaf and mashed potato sandwiches. Once, a jar of capers, a package of crackers, and my aunt Ann's red pepper jelly. Roast beef starts to look really good.

"You don't even look anymore, do you?" It's an accusation, not a question.

"Sometimes I can finish it before I figure out what it is. If I eat fast enough, sometimes," I say, still chewing, "I can eat the whole thing without really tasting it."

I peel back the top layer of bread. The brown spread is most likely peanut butter. The red chunks are probably peppers. The little white squares have to be tofu. My mother thinks adding peanut butter to anything makes it authentically Thai. I don't believe that anyone in Thailand eats peanut butter, pepper, and tofu sandwiches. At least not on white bread.

"You could make your own lunch," David suggests, handing me a half of one half of his sandwich. I've noticed that he is more willing to share the ham sandwiches than the roast beef. Not sure what to make of this fact. I'd feel worse about my mother still packing my lunch for me if she did a better job at it.

School

There is nothing about history that requires me to do anything other than look alert, which I can do without paying any attention at all. The same five people answer all of Ms. Kalikowski's questions, and she prefers a lively class of five with twelve onlookers to trying to get the rest of us to participate. Sometimes I surprise her by raising my hand. She always looks pleased—partly, I think, because when I do say something it is relevant.

School

"Do you need a ride home today?"

"Always."

I follow David to the parking lot, the way I have for most of the last year, as if nothing at all was different.

CHAPTER 5

Godless, Homosexual, Vegetarian Communists

Will she skip ski trips if he slips tongue tricks?

Over the last six months, David has become our taxi service. Since about October, he's been giving me, Carrie, and Carrie's best friend, M.C., a ride home several times a week, and he still does on days when he doesn't have baseball practice. We don't even ask anymore. Carrie and M.C. wait for us in the parking lot so they won't be too identified with us. We are not the cool juniors, but Carrie decided that the bus is way too ninth-grade and David has a car.

David doesn't seem to mind. At least he doesn't say he minds. I'm not sure what he gets out of the deal.

Sometimes Carrie makes us stop on the way home. We need french fries, we need gum, we need some shade of lip stuff, and the world always depends on us having it before we get home. Home is clearly some form of dungeon. David shrugs, we stop. David shrugs a lot. It took me a while to realize that the shrugs mean something.

A short list of David's non-verbal vocabulary:

1) Shrug = okay. It is used to indicate that he is willing to go along, but only because you asked. It's a sort of "I don't care either way."

2) Pulling glasses = not so okay, but also a sign that he probably doesn't have any choice, so he will go along with it anyway.

3) Rubbing the top of his nose. He uses his whole hand for this maneuver. It means "I am really uncomfortable with this suggestion," but unless there is an easy way out, he will go along with it anyway.

4) Staring at his feet. If he is driving, the same effect is accomplished by staring robotically ahead and not responding. This is an attempt to convince you not to ask whatever you are about to ask. Bottom line: he will go along with it anyway.

Usually Carrie and M.C. ignore us, which is just fine. But today Carrie taps me on the shoulder from the backseat.

"I have a question. You're guys," she says. I don't immediately answer because I assume that our guyhood is not the question. "So give us a guy opinion."

"Sure," I say. I hate agreeing before I know what it is I'm agreeing to.

Carrie then launches into a very long story. It begins hypothetically, something about "this girl," who "may or may not" have done something with "this guy" on this camping trip, or maybe it was skiing, anyway, it wasn't here, but he came back and told everyone about it, even though there wasn't much to tell about it because they hardly did anything at all. So if she didn't really do anything, but she did something, and now that they're back she doesn't want to do anything at all, this is his problem, not hers, right?

I start to ask who, but I can tell from the punching in the backseat who the story is about and that the right answer is of course his problem, not hers.

"So you'd be willing to go out with someone who you knew this about, wouldn't you? If you liked her, you wouldn't care who she kissed on some camping trip."

If I say I wouldn't go out with her, then I've just implied that I wouldn't want to date an indiscriminate kisser, which feels all wrong particularly since I'm pretty sure I'd be in favor of it if it involved my mouth. If I say yes, I have admitted that I would be willing to ask her out, although I guess not as the real M.C., just as an abstract M.C.

"Sure, yeah, of course. Yeah."

"See," Carrie says, turning back to the less hypothetical M.C. "Even my brother would go out with you. What about you, David?"

"I'm saving myself for marriage."

Perhaps popular people pick a pepperoni pizza

Carrie convinces us that we need to stop for pizza.

"I'm not hungry," David argues.

"So?" Carrie answers.

"So, why do I need to eat pizza at 3:30 in the afternoon?"

The real answer is because Carrie told us we had to, but she tells David it is because she and M.C. so value his companionship and wit, which amounts to the same thing. David shrugs, we get pizza. He sits with M.C. and I sit with Carrie and it could be a date except David is gay and I'm sitting next to my sister.

We agree that a whole pizza is cheaper than slices for four people but David doesn't eat pepperoni.

"You're joking, right?" Carrie never knows quite what to make of David.

"No, I don't eat pepperoni."

"But you do eat pizza?"

"Yes, just not pepperoni."

"I didn't realize you're a vegetarian," M.C. says brightly. "My older sister is a vegetarian, except she eats fish. And chicken. And turkey at Thanksgiving. And sometimes bacon cheeseburgers." I think she's joking, but she keeps a straight face. She's a little like David; I can never tell when she's being serious. The difference between the two is that David never smiles when he's making a joke and M.C. smiles even when she isn't.

"I'm not a vegetarian," David says calmly. "I just don't eat pepperoni."

"I don't get it," Carrie says. "Everyone eats pepperoni pizza. It is one of those things you can count on. Are you sure you're an American? What kind of pizza do you like?"

29

"Pineapple."

We order pizza with black olives. I don't like black olives, but I'm not willing to make it an issue.

David dating data

"Is David dating anyone?" Carrie asks me, pretty much as soon as we walk in the door. David had offered to drop M.C. off at her house, but she decided she would do her homework here. Currently that involves sitting in front of our television in the playroom. Carrie, meanwhile, has cornered me in the kitchen.

"Don't tell me you're interested in David."

"Not personally, no. But is he?"

"I don't think so."

"Wouldn't you know?"

"Maybe."

"What about Mariel?"

"They're friends."

Carrie cocks one eyebrow. That ability must be genetic; why can't I do it? "Really?" she asks. "They seem awfully friendly."

"I think they're just friends."

"You think?"

"I'm pretty sure."

"But he hasn't said anything about her to you?"

"We've never talked about her."

"What do you talk about? He's your best friend, you're

in almost all of the same classes, you eat lunch with him every day—don't you know anything about him?"

"I know what he eats for lunch."

Loathsome Louis longs to munch much lovely lunch

David spends too much time at lunch pitching possible essay titles at me. This is not for my benefit; he does it before every major assignment. David starts with the title, then writes a paper to fit it.

" 'Joad as Toad: Character in *The Grapes of Wrath.*' "

David likes colons. You can hear them in his pause. He looks to me for a reaction.

"Possible. Nice rhyme. Subtitle needs work."

He nods and looks solemn again.

" 'Mapquest: Map and Quest—Just Where Were the Joads Going?' "

"Better."

There is a pause before the next pitch, and I look up to find Louis behind my chair. Louis never arrives, he just appears. For someone his size, that's an accomplishment.

"Hello, Louis," David says, placing his apple core back in his brown paper lunch bag. In defiance of all social norms, he always carries a traditional brown bag, which emerges every day from his backpack unwrinkled and stands on the table with remarkable posture for a near-empty paper sack. It's some sort of statement, because for most people the goal is to make the fact that you brought your lunch look as unintentional as possible. The food should look like you just happened to find it—hey, there's a tuna fish sandwich in my pocket. There are a few categories of people, mostly girls, who can get away with actual lunchboxes, but only if they can convey proper irony.

"Ditchell, Mavid."

Louis frequently joins us at lunch, which is surprising because David and I are the only juniors who have early lunch. In theory, Louis should be in class now. But here he is again. He pulls up a chair and places it right alongside David's, leg to leg. David scoots a little to the left to mitigate the personal space invasion.

Sitting next to David, I realize that he and Louis are almost the same size. But while David isn't someone you would easily pick out of a lineup of teenagers, Louis is someone you would notice immediately. He's a lot like David, only more so. Both are taller than me, but not really tall. On David, the height makes him look average. Louis is a little chubbier, with a rounder face and enough weight to make him bulky, but not really fat. His height makes him seem big. David's hair is blond, but not pale blond, or Swedish blond or beach blond—just mostly blond with enough streaks of brown to make the blondness less noticeable. Louis is fair as well, but his hair is almost yellow, and there is something beacon-like about his head that makes him easy to spot walking down the hall. And then there's the grin. David doesn't really smile much. He might enjoy things, but deadpan is as funny as he gets. Louis is always wearing a very wide, very happy grin. It isn't really a friendly grin, but it sure makes him look like he's enjoying himself.

Louis picks up David's lunch bag and shakes it a little. "Not even any chips left! Selfish bastard. So tell me, Mitch Hell, have you been keeping tabs on how some of these freshgirls have become much more fresh and less menly? Where did those tits come from? You guys haven't noticed at all, have you? Just squeaky background noise. More important things to focus on, huh? Like your sister's best friend. Not too developed, but close at hand. How close were your hands?"

"Louis, what are you talking about?" I finally ask. Louis should come with subtitles.

"Pizza. Double-dating with your sister. Little odd, backseat-frontseat kind of thing. I guess it's kosher, as long as you don't try reliving those bathtub moments from when you were three. Of course, if my sister was Carrie . . ."

"How did you know we went out for pizza?"

"Usual methods. Tire tracks. Surveillance cameras. Mozzarella on your breath. Zach works there in the kitchen making pizza."

"Louis," David says, checking his watch, "maybe you should try to get a life of your own. Start simple. A hobby. Or showing up for class."

"Evade all you want, but it makes me proud when two eunuchs such as yourselves take those first teeny steps toward manhood. But you're right. I'm probably late for French. Or maybe physics."

"The scary thing," David says as we watch Louis leave, "is that he is ranked second in our class." He checks his watch again. David doesn't trust the cafeteria clocks. "Wallman time."

"I figured out what a green screen is," I tell him as we get up to leave. "There's definitely one in the lab. We can do some really cool things, but we'll have to convince one of the senior trolls to help. It involves some computer program I've never heard of, but it doesn't look impossible. I'm going to try to get in some time after school— Wallman said it was fine."

"You're starting to scare me," David says, tossing his lunch bag in the trash can by the door. He doesn't sound scared.

"Oh, come on. We're on a roll."

"Have you started your English paper?"

"No."

"Have you finished reading the book?"

"No."

"Have you started reading the book?"

"I've tried. I just can't do it. I can't get past page seven."

David gives a little grunting noise of disapproval. Two freshman girls pass us in the hall. Louis is right. Now that spring has arrived and they aren't layered in coats and sweaters, the ninth graders definitely have more to show.

"David," I ask as we turn the corner and walk down the long hallway to the film lab. "I know that you aren't hooking up with Mariel . . ."

David stops walking and turns toward me. I have set off the perimeter defenses.

"And I know why you aren't, but theoretically, if you were, which I know you're not, would you have told me?"

David doesn't quite know what to do with that question. He pushes his glasses back toward the bridge of his nose.

"Yes," he says.

"What if it wasn't Mariel?"

He pauses again, considering. Finally, he shrugs. "Probably."

"So, nothing has happened?"

The door opens and a stream of sophomores passes us by. He waits them out before he says no, as if that one syllable would reveal some secret he doesn't want anyone to overhear.

CHAPTER 6

The Masturbation Chapter

To the red country and part of the gray country of Oklahoma, the last rains came gently, and they did not cut the scarred earth.

I'm almost asleep by the end of the first line. I have decided to start the book over again because I can't remember one thing that happened in the seven pages I read. There was dust, lots of dust, I got that, but the whys and wherefroms were a little fuzzy. Maybe it wasn't important. Like why there were two countries in Oklahoma. Part of the problem with a book like this is trying to figure out what is important information and what isn't.

Gophers and ant lions started small avalanches.

I don't know what a gopher or an ant lion looks like. I don't even know what an ant lion is. I suppose I could look it up, but how important can it be? There is not an essay topic on ant lions in *The Grapes of Wrath*. Keep going, keep going.

And as the sharp sun struck day after day, the leaves of the young corn became less stiff and erect . . .

Stiff and erect. Is it just me or is that a little suggestive? Maybe because I'm reading in bed. I am not currently stiff and erect. Was Steinbeck gay? Fitzgerald was the one with the goofy wife—Steinbeck had a little mustache, I think. That wouldn't make him gay.

. . . they bent at a curve at first, and then, as the central ribs of strength grew weak, each leaf tilted downwards.

Poor leaves.

Is this what I've become? I'm spending my time lying in bed thinking about penises? Oh, God, maybe I *am* gay. I mean, it would be okay if I was. Sort of. But it would be a surprise. How could I not know I was gay? I know I'm not in touch with my feelings, but I'm pretty clear about my hormones. Denial wouldn't cover it. I could be bi, maybe. That would almost be cool. But it would be sort of half-gay. Mitchell, you're being an idiot. Having a gay friend does not make you gay. Even if you've never done anything with a girl. On the other hand, I've never done anything with a guy either. David says I throw a baseball like a girl. David can actually throw baseballs, so maybe that's irrelevant.

Read, Mitchell. Read.

The men sat still in the doorways of their houses,
their hands were busy with sticks and little rocks.
The men sat still—thinking—figuring.

I think I would rather be playing with my stick and my little rocks than reading this book. There is nothing so far in any of the first four pages I've read that feels even remotely related to my life. In the last eleven years I have swallowed more books like this than I can count. I can't get this one down.

⊚   ⊙   ⊚

I close the book and drop it back onto the dirty laundry I still haven't cleaned up. When did my mom stop coming in and cleaning my room? Is it dangerous to sleep next to so many smelly clothes? Isn't there like bacteria and stuff in there? Why do I always have questions like this before I go to sleep? I need an answer.

In the dark, in my bed, I give myself an erection test. One by one I imagine every student in my English class. If I only have erections for the females, I'm straight. It's really the only way to tell. I start with Simone, who doesn't get much of a reaction, unless I imagine her without her shirt, which is surprisingly easy given that I've never seen her without one. Louis, thank God, is an erection killer and Thad scores in the negatives as well. It is a little too creepy to think about Mariel without her shirt—it feels like an invasion of privacy. Danielle sits next to

Mariel. Danielle is as far as I get. I reach into the crack between my bed and the wall for the old T-shirt that I need to find a way to wash soon.

In the dust there were drop craters where the rain had fallen and clean splashes on the corn, and that was all.

CHAPTER 7

Hypotheticals

Scenario 1: Three guys walk into a . . .

Say three guys are standing in a hall waiting for the class before them to file out so they can go in. A female student wearing jeans walks past them. The jeans aren't obscenely tight but fit nicely and emphasize the roundness of her backside. What is the proper reaction?

This is not a hypothetical question. Louis, David, and I are standing in the hallway, waiting to go into chemistry. Danielle, on the way to her locker (she will show up for class fashionably late), passes by us with a slight nod that might be an acknowledgment that she knows who we are. I look at the floor, immediately flustered. Louis taps me so I can see that he has turned to stare at her butt as she walks down the hall.

"Admit it, you'd give your left nut to bang her," he says with an exaggerated sigh.

David clears his throat. "Wouldn't that be counter-productive?"

Louis gives David a blank look.

David clears his throat again. "I mean, without a left nut, wouldn't it be hard to bang her?"

"I think you might be able to . . . bang somebody with only one nut," I suggest. "I don't think you need both."

Louis can't decide whether we're stupid or joking, so he concentrates on Danielle's retreating behind. "You guys fags or something?"

At some point when you are still in elementary school, someone teaches you the word "faggot," the noun meaning a bundle of sticks. For me, it was fourth grade. We were reading an adaptation of *A Connecticut Yankee in King Arthur's Court* and whoever was doing the adapting didn't feel the need to adapt that word into something we wouldn't giggle about. I think most of us had no idea why we giggled when the faggots were brought forth to burn Hank Morgan, but it sounded dirty and dangerous. We already knew you could use "bitch" if you were talking about dogs, and "ass" was a donkey, and we tried our best to come up with sentences where we could get away with using those words in front of adults. But even then we knew "faggot" was different.

Our fourth-grade teacher, Ms. Baker, was a theatrical woman with too much hair, which sometimes she piled on her head and other times she wore in a long braid down her back. The braid was a swirl of brown and gray, but she wore jeans and played kickball with us at recess. For Ms. Baker the classroom was a stage and we performed regularly, so it was not a surprise when she assigned us scenes from *A Connecticut Yankee* to turn into little skits. I can't remember which scene I was in, but I do remember that three or four of the boys were given the burning scene. The scenes were never elaborate, we always mimed the props, and it was often a little difficult to tell what was going on. Louis was King Arthur, I think, and I can't recall who played Hank, but I do remember that at one point he yelled very loudly, "Bring in the faggots," and Thad and Glenn skipped in together pretending to be holding wood. General mayhem followed.

What did we understand about this joke? Enough, I guess, to link the skipping and the two boys together to the word "faggot." They skipped in and we called them faggots and we thought it was the funniest thing we had seen in a classroom since Douglas farted loudly during a quiz in third grade.

◉   ◉   ◉

A week ago Louis's comment would not have even registered. But suddenly the word means something to me. How am I supposed to respond?

1) I could tell Louis, in a shrill voice, that I feel strongly that his use of the word "fag" is derogatory and insensitive. Louis would, of course, immediately apologize and never use the word again. He would also never suspect that one of

us is actually gay or mercilessly make fun of me for the rest of my high-school career.

2) I could respond with some witty comeback. That would require me to think of some witty comeback.

3) I could punch him for calling me a fag. It would be an overreaction and I've never punched anyone before and he outweighs me by a good twenty pounds and if he decided to punch me back I could end up in detention or the hospital, but I wouldn't just be letting it go.

4) I could just let it go.

I just let it go. So does David.

Scenario 2: Say there was this teacher . . .

There is something strange going on with M.C. First of all, she signed up to do scenery for the play. M.C. has always been theatrical, but never really into theater. She is not a techie. The techies are a small, fiercely independent tribe at White Day, very alternative, well-pierced, dread-locked, clothed in black. M.C. sometimes comes to school wearing a large straw hat. *She is not a techie.*

On Tuesday, David doesn't have practice but M.C. isn't waiting for us with Carrie in the parking lot. Stranded by herself in the backseat of David's car, Carrie looks a little lost.

David is innocent enough to ask, "Where's M.C.?"

"Painting flats."

"Why?" There is no sarcasm in David's voice. It just isn't one of those things he would ever volunteer to do.

"For the play. They're scenery." I know that this answer means "Leave me alone." David, however, doesn't.

"I know what they are, why is M.C. doing it?"

Carrie squirms. She has lost a little of her normal confident swagger. She could say she doesn't know, but we wouldn't believe her.

"She's got it for one of the tech-heads?" David asks with a smile, which is as close as he will get to a wink.

Carrie nods.

"Which one?"

"Curtis."

David looks at me. I'm trying to make sense out of it too.

"We have a tech-head named Curtis?" I ask, hoping that someone I don't know is working crew. Mr. Curtis, our English teacher, is the faculty advisor for the drama club, but . . .

"*Mr.* Curtis."

This shuts both David and me up. We don't mention M.C. again for the rest of the ride home. Once home, however, I corner Carrie in the living room. This requires some explanation.

"She has a crush. You've had crushes on teachers."

I can't decide whether the "you" is generic or really me, but since for the last two years I have had the same fairly lurid fantasy about Ms. St. Claire, one of the art teachers, posing nude for class, I don't contest the accusation.

"But Curtis?"

"He's young, disheveled, he's got a rugged, intellectual look. Handsome in that sort of way. Nice butt. Sort of M.C.'s type, if you think about it."

Is Curtis young? Does he really have a nice butt? I have never thought about Curtis's butt. I wonder if I have a nice butt. Has anyone ever noticed my rear end?

"But he's a . . . a teacher."

"Very observant, Mitchell. She has a crush on a teacher. He's twenty-eight, she's sixteen. Stranger things have happened."

"Has something happened?" I am totally disturbed by this idea. I can't even get around the idea that she would think of Curtis in that way. I'm stunned.

"Relax, Cotton Mather, nothing has happened." Carrie sounds dismissive, but she looks worried. She isn't liking this either.

We don't discuss it, but it is now on my mind. I go to my room and purposefully don't fantasize about naked art teachers, and particularly not about Curtis's butt. M.C. comes over after dinner and I can't look at her. She and Carrie head off to the mall, and for once I want to go with them so I can listen to the conversation. This would count as the first time I have ever been interested in their conversation.

On Wednesday, I make the mistake of asking David.

I try to just work it into the conversation. Casually, as we walk back from lunch and no one's around, I ask about his German test, what he thought of the speaker at morning assembly, and whether he thought Mr. Curtis was handsome, you know, in that sort of rugged, intellectual kind of way.

David looks at me for a long time, like he's waiting for the punch line. His face remains blank, but I can see what's working behind that look. He knows that I've asked him this because he's gay, and therefore now an expert on male attractiveness. He knows that my asking is my attempt to acknowledge this fact that we haven't mentioned since his lunch announcement last week. This is my way of reassuring him that it's all cool, that we can have conversations like this. Only we can't. It's a little too personal, a little too forced, not something he wants to discuss with me. He licks his lips and tugs at his glasses and says, "No."

"I don't think so either," I say, way too quickly. It feels like someone has moved our lockers since yesterday. They aren't usually this far away.

"You know, I was thinking," I say, trying very hard to change the topic. "I might stay late and work on our film. I had some ideas. Would that be okay?"

"Sure. Knock yourself out."

"You have baseball today, right?"

"You need a ride home?"

"Just this once."

Scenario 3: What if two mild-mannered honors students . . .

David meets me in the editing room after baseball practice. I have spent the last three and a half hours putting our film together. There are a few parts David hasn't seen yet. I am particularly proud of my *Grapes of Wrath*–inspired dust bowl scene. I talked one of the maintenance staff into letting me empty the contents of the vacuum cleaner bag onto the floor. He gave me a look like maybe I was off my meds, but he stayed and watched as I dropped all of the major characters one by one into the pile, which produced wonderful plumes of debris. When I was done he just shook his head sadly while I helped him clean it back up. After I added the screams to the soundtrack, it became one of my favorite sequences.

"You know," David says, watching it through the second time, "Wallman is going to love this. It has everything he loves about movies: senseless violence, lots of blood, and you even got sex in there—well, not real sex but a good nude scene. They were naked in the opening, right?"

I fast-backward to the opening.

"It was a little hard to get them to look naked."

"Eve's nipples look like buttons . . ."

"That's because they are buttons."

"Oh. That would explain it. What are we using for a title?" David sits in the chair next to me and plays with the dials on the mixer.

"We still need to make a title sequence, but how does 'Steinbeck Sucks' sound to you?"

"Great—a tribute to your English essay."

"Which I still haven't written."

"You know," David says thoughtfully, "if we called it 'Biblical Themes in *The Grapes of Wrath*,' we could turn it in to Curtis. We have, like, eight Steinbeck references— nine if you notice that the devil sort of looks like the picture of him on the back of the book."

"Hey, why not? What's the worst thing that can happen?"

"We fail English. We are forced to endure ridicule and humiliation in front of our peers. Stress-induced hypertension and eventually death."

"I mean besides that."

CHAPTER 8

Way Too Much Whining and Some Thoughts on Pissing

5:32 a.m.

It is 5:32. In less than two minutes, my alarm will go off. I hate waking up before the alarm.

I feel defeated. Absolutely, unquestionably, utterly, and hopelessly defeated. I do not want to go to school. I do not want to get out of bed. I can't imagine how I will get through the next sixty or so years of my life. I cannot write this paper.

It's just a paper. A stupid standard five-paragraph essay. The same stupid five-paragraph essay I have written approximately every two weeks since fifth grade. My self-esteem does not depend on whether this particular paper is good or bad. I have other sources of self-esteem. Not that I can come up with any right this moment, but I'm sure there is something about me that I can . . .

Maybe not. Maybe I am really as worthless as I feel right now. Mr. Rogers might have liked me just the way I am, but I certainly don't. Everybody is special in their own way—how many times did we get that lecture? Followed by the same inane list: some are good at sports, some are artistic, some sing, some can do complicated math equations in their heads and will go on to win Nobel Prizes.

Let's review: I can't play sports, I'm not artistic, I can't sing, and I can barely add single digits in my head. The Nobel committee isn't likely to call. I'm good at this litany of self-pity. Do they give Nobel Prizes for whining? I cannot write this paper.

I can deal with the fact that I'm a hopeless dweeboid and that my grandmother, who is eighty-two and pushes an aluminum walker, has a more active social life than I do, but the one thing dweeboids are supposed to be good at is homework. I'm even a failure at being a dweeboid.

I cannot write this paper.

It is 5:34. The radio clicks, the static starts. I sit up, both feet on the ground. I stare at the offensive plastic cube for a full thirty seconds before turning it off.

I should have read the book over the weekend. And I really tried. At least I sort of tried. I opened it twice. It's not like it was the only assignment I had to finish. And Monday, there was a chem test to study for. What was I going to do, blow that off?

Last night I sat in front of the computer and held my hands over the keys. I typed my name, the date, and the title of the paper, erased it, typed it again. I changed the font from Times New Roman to Courier to Arial. I considered adding my middle name, added it, changed my mind, deleted it. After several hours of not writing the paper, I set my alarm and went to bed, telling myself I would deal with it in the morning. Now it is morning. To be more specific, it is 5:36.

I pull myself out of bed. Still in my boxer shorts, I sit bare-chested at the computer.

I cannot write this paper.

6:14 a.m.

"Mitchell—what time is it?"

"6:15."

"In the morning?"

"Yes."

There is silence on the other end of the line. It is an unhappy silence. I don't think David is eager to talk to me right now.

"Did I wake you up?" I ask, trying to sound surprised.

"Not directly. My mother just did that. To tell me you were on the phone."

"Sorry. What time do you usually get up?"

"My alarm goes off in about ten minutes."

So why are you so grumpy? A lousy ten minutes of sleep. I'm having a crisis here.

"If you had a cell phone, I could have called you without waking up your parents." David doesn't own a cell phone because he doesn't want anyone to be able to reach him wherever he is. I've suggested, any number of times, that he could screen his calls, leave it on vibrate or even silent. He has yet to see the utility.

"My parents were already awake. Mitchell, why are you calling me at 6:15 in the morning?"

"It's already 6:25. You'd have been awake now anyway."

"Mitchell."

"Have you written your paper?"

"The one that's due today?" As if he didn't know.

"Yes."

"Yes."

"Don't turn it in. We'll turn in our film instead."

David pauses. "You didn't write your paper."

"Not exactly," I admit. "Well, not at all. But your idea about turning in the film . . ."

"Was a joke," David says slowly. Nothing about the way he says "joke" sounds funny.

"But I've been thinking. It really could work. It's creative, it's different, it's expressive, it's already mostly finished." I can hear the skepticism in David's silence. "I'm going to talk to Curtis before class. If he says no, I'll admit I didn't write the paper. If he goes for it, we're golden. This has to be better than whatever you wrote about."

I hear a shuffling noise that sounds like David is getting out of bed. Has he been lying in his bed this whole time?

Maybe sitting. He is on the move now. I just hope he's not going to the bathroom. I will not talk to someone in the bathroom, even if I woke them up. No, it sounds more like the kitchen. He's pouring himself something. Coffee? Juice?

"Mitchell," he says in his best why-is-your-brain-up your-butt voice. "There are a couple of problems with this plan." A pause, and I hear him take a slurp of whatever he's poured. "First of all, I wrote a damn good paper on the evolution of Joad's ethical sensibility . . ."

"Nice title."

"Thank you."

"But no colons."

"You noticed. I'm branching out. Second, our film has almost nothing whatsoever to do with *The Grapes of Wrath*, which you might not have noticed since you haven't read the book . . ."

"I read some."

"How much?"

"Three chapters. But I skipped ahead to the end so I know how it turns out. Or at least I read the last two pages where she, um . . . does that thing."

"Third," David continues, unimpressed, "it isn't a three-to-five-page paper about *The Grapes of Wrath*."

"So does that mean you don't think it's a good idea?"

"Feel free to turn it in, just don't put my name on it. I have to go take a piss now."

We hang up. I look at the blank page with a heading and no title. I never use the word "piss." I never "take a piss." I'm not sure where I would take it to. I pee. I need to learn to piss. I am not writing this paper.

6:45 a.m.

I spend the next twenty minutes making an impressive but tasteful label for the DVD and a matching insert for its cheap plastic case. I place it carefully in my backpack and go downstairs for some cereal. Our dog joins me for breakfast, staring at me as I search the kitchen. All we have left is an off-brand granola, but I'm not going to let that spoil my day. I'm feeling brave, nearly reckless. Rebel without an English paper. David, I decide while munching the stale granola, is being unreasonably sensible. But then again, he always is. Never mind, I'll go it alone. I'm ready to talk to Curtis. After all, what's the worst thing that can happen?

CHAPTER 9

Jerks, Myoclonic and Otherwise

Curtis

English class. 8:17. Curtis, Mr. Curtis, Mr. Albert P. Curtis, M.A., sits on his stool at the front of the room regarding us with a suspicious glare.

Curtis is dressed in his geeky teacher uniform of khakis (slightly worn at the cuffs) and a button-down (with both old and current coffee stains). We slouch in our slug wear: jeans, T-shirts, sweats. Our faces are pierced, our hair is purposefully unruly, and all our clothes are too large—except Danielle's, which are a little too tight.

Curtis begins to lecture. Instantly he becomes background noise. He waves his arms about, gestures with sincerity. As we drift into our own little worlds, his voice becomes more and more strident. There is something he is trying to say.

"The subjective experience of the character is portrayed through the conscious manipulation of point of view."

Danielle stares at her notebook. She doesn't doodle. She doesn't take notes. Her notebook is blank. She examines her nails. They are a subtle shade of green with an elegant white swirl across each nail. Glamour does not come cheap. She smooths her skirt, touches her hair, and, suddenly aware of her posture, sits up straighter. She sneaks a look at the cell phone placed strategically on top of her purse to see how many messages she has accumulated during class. She glances around to see if anyone is watching her. She returns to staring at her notebook.

"Characterization." Curtis writes the word on the board. A few of us write it in our notebooks. "The delineation of the particular qualities, features, and traits of a fictional person, conveyed primarily, in decent novels, through the character's actions and dialogue . . ."

Louis is giving himself a nosebleed. It's a trick he doesn't overuse, so he must really want out of this class. The first time I remember him doing it was in fifth grade, as a way of postponing a geography test when we were supposed to have memorized all of the state capitals. He first tugs out some of the deeper nose hairs, then taps the side of his nose, up near the bridge. It takes about ten minutes, and then there's a gush of very red blood. I've never wanted a nosebleed badly enough to try it.

The gush comes. Louis catches it on his shirt. I hope he has to do his own laundry. He raises his hand.

"Excuse me, Mr. Curtis, sir?" Louis calls all the teachers sir or ma'am.

"Are you bleeding?" Curtis asks. He sounds a little shaken. He's not one to question the obvious.

"Yes sir, I'm sorry. I get nosebleeds. It's a puberty thing, sir. May I go to the bathroom?"

"Please," says Curtis.

Still holding his shirt to his nose, Louis uses his free hand to grab his backpack, slings it over his shoulder, and leaves the room. He's not coming back. On the way out he pats Thad on the back, leaving a bloody handprint.

" 'Character' is a noun. 'Characterize' is a verb. Both are derived from the Greek word . . ." And here Curtis stops to write something even more unintelligible than his usual handwriting. It looks as if it starts with an x. I assume he is now writing in Greek. "The word meant to mark, to distinguish . . ."

I drop my pencil. Well, "drop" would be an understatement. I don't just drop my pencil. I fling my pencil. I hurl it across the room. For several minutes I've been doing that nodding thing, where you start to fall asleep, then catch yourself just as your head moves forward and then you jerk back up suddenly. Fourth, maybe fifth nod, I jerk back up and my pencil flies across the room. It lands in front of Curtis, perfectly into the little space between him and the class, the demilitarized zone, the no-man's-land. Everyone looks up, then back.

If I had been quick, I could have looked around as if I also didn't know where the pencil came from. If I had been Louis, I would have tapped some schlep next to me (it probably would have been me), and said, "Good shot, dickhead." If I had been cool, I could shrug it off. Big deal.

As I am me, my face immediately drains of all color. My eyes feel moist, my hands clammy. I sit on my hands. I stare straight ahead, into the oncoming headlights of Curtis's impending anger. I can't breathe. Everyone is watching me. I can feel myself expand, grow larger, fill up all of the empty spaces in the room.

Curtis picks up the pencil and walks the three rows back to my desk.

"This yours?" he asks.

I nod.

He places it on top of my open notebook, next to my doodle of a vaguely Curtis-like person impaled on a giant pencil.

"Try holding on tighter," he suggests without any inflection, and then he launches into a soliloquy on stream of consciousness.

Beware anything that is too easy

David is sort of waiting for me at my locker. He always looks as if he just happens to be there when I get there, not like he's waiting for me.

"Myoclonic jerk," he says cheerfully.

"What did I do to you?"

"No, dumbshit, in class, the pencil thing. It's called a myoclonic jerk. It's a medical term. Aren't you a doctor's son?"

"It doesn't mean I know anything."

"We talked about it in biology last year."

I sort of remember biology last year, but nothing this specific.

"It's the sudden convulsion people sometimes have right before they fall asleep." David then does his imitation of a myoclonic jerk. I look around to see if anyone is watching.

"Don't do that again. You look like you're having a fit."

David shrugs. "Three inches farther and you would have nailed him in the gonads." He then smiles. "So, I thought you were going to ask him."

"I didn't want to do it in front of everyone. I'll go back at break."

At break, I find Curtis in his room, sitting at his desk reading a copy of *The New Yorker*. Doesn't he have papers to grade or something? Is it legal for him to read a magazine during school hours? He looks a little startled when I knock on the open door. Maybe he isn't used to talking to students outside of class. Maybe I'm nervous.

"Can I talk to you about the paper . . . the paper that was due today, the *Grapes of Wrath* paper?"

"I know which paper was due today. No, you can't have an extension. It has been on the syllabus since the beginning of the semester." He returns his attention to his magazine.

"I . . . um, don't need an extension." At least not if you buy this idea. "I don't know if you know this about me"—you don't, almost no one does—"but I'm interested in Claymation and I have been making films. Claymation films." Films, not cartoons. "I had this idea while reading *The Grapes of Wrath*"—or at least looking at the cover—"that I could, well . . . what I tried to do was capture something about the novel . . . I made a film and I have been working on it for a while and . . ."

I have his attention. He has now closed *The New Yorker* and would be looking me in the eyes, if I actually looked up. He seems oddly alert, like a small rodent that's heard a sudden noise. His nose might have twitched. He is really trying to figure out what it is I am trying to say. In class he rarely lets anyone finish a sentence. He gives the constant impression that he already knows whatever you were about to say and has already decided that it isn't worth listening to.

"I can tell you are trying to tell me something, or possibly ask me something."

"Ask. I was asking."

"And this film, about the book . . ."

"It's a sort of project."

"Instead of a paper."

"Yeah."

"Sure." He smiles. I stand there and stare at him. Seeing how I haven't responded, he continues, "I like initiative and creativity. I'd be happy to watch a . . . Claymation . . . ?"

"Like Gumby. A cartoon, sort of."

"Sounds great. Do you have it with you? Because, whatever it is, it is still due today."

I pull it out of my bag. He looks at the cover and hands it back to me.

"I can shift things around a little, why don't we show it on Friday right after we wrap up the *Grapes* unit?"

I'm not quite prepared for this reaction. "Do you want to preview it first?"

"No, I trust you."

"Okay, thanks," I say, and walk slowly back to my locker, thinking, "No. Don't trust me." I have made a seven-minute cartoon with naked clay figures being tortured in various ways and I am about to turn it in as an essay on Steinbeck. I don't feel particularly trustworthy. Maybe I could change schools. Maybe I could convince my parents to move. We could go to a new state. Oklahoma. We could move to Oklahoma.

"So what did he say?"

M.C. seems to be standing between me and my locker. I am used to seeing her Post-it notes above my lock, which are her way of letting me know she expects David to give her a ride home, but I'm not used to seeing her stand here in person. I have never asked why I get the notes and not

David, but I assume it has something to do with my being Carrie's brother.

"I'm thinking of moving to Oklahoma. Would you like to elope with me and live in Oklahoma?"

"Too flat. What did he say?" M.C. arches her eyebrow. A clear physical question mark. M.C. may be one of the more animated people I know.

"He said yes. He wants to show it on Friday."

"I knew he would, he's so cool."

Has someone changed the meaning of the word "cool"?

"It doesn't matter, I'm not going to do it. I'm moving to Oklahoma."

"Not before Friday. It will be great." M.C. does this little wiggle thing she always does when she's happy. It's like she's smiling with her whole body. I can't figure out why she's enjoying this so much.

"Gotta run," she says, leaning into the words. "See ya."

I watch her walk down the hall. I have known M.C. for at least nine years. I know her family, the name of her goldfish, her PSAT score, and the colors of most of her shoes. I still have no idea what is going on behind her freckled forehead.

Maybe I just don't have any idea about what's going on, period

Louis is sitting with David at lunch. He has already appropriated David's chips. David is defending his sandwich and apple by holding one in each hand and never placing them on the table. Louis looks up as if he is surprised to see me here.

"Well, Mitch, Mitch Wells, join us. We were just discussing underwear."

I'm guessing David didn't choose the topic. He waits for me to sit down and then tries to pretend Louis isn't there. It is a strategy that never works.

"I was thinking . . . ," David tells me.

"Me too," Louis interrupts. "Hurts, doesn't it? I think there's surgery they can do now to prevent that."

"I was thinking about talking to Wallman . . . ," David began again.

"Not me. I was thinking about Ms. Kalikowski. Better legs than Wallman. In fact, I was having happy thoughts all the way through history class. Whenever she wears her tennis dress to class it always gives me happy thoughts." Ms. Kalikowski, in addition to being our history teacher, also coaches tennis. Often she changes into her whites halfway through the day. She is youngish for a teacher, cheerful, and maybe even cute, but I don't think she would be the object of so much discussion if she didn't wear a short tennis skirt to teach American history.

David shakes his head and waits for more, but Louis appears to have finished his thought. So he starts again. "I was thinking . . ."

"About kilts? Me too. I've been thinking a lot about

kilts." Louis pauses for our reaction, which doesn't impress him. "You see, while I was having my happy thoughts about Ms. K bending over to pick up the chalk, it occurred to me that men should wear skirts. Women don't need them, there's nothing in their pants that needs extra room in the middle of class. But a man, now—for those twenty or thirty times a day a happy thought overcomes him, he needs some room to expand into. Some of us, of course, need more room than others. So, I decided, kilts."

"You're going to start wearing kilts?" David asks, giving up.

"Which is why I wanted to talk undies. Boxers under kilts? Boxer briefs? Kangaroo pockets? Or nothing at all? Yeah, nothing, right? I thought so. But do you think kilts rub—would the wool be rough? I hate to leave you with that thought, but somewhere there is a class where I am notably absent. And I have sworn to figure out which one it is before the end of the year. Are you going to eat that?"

Louis points to the bag of cold leftover pasta that I have pulled out of my lunch bag.

"All yours."

"Thanks."

"I don't want to think about Louis chafing under a kilt," I say, after Louis and my lunch leave.

"Not a pretty thought," David agrees.

I wait for David to ask, but he doesn't, so I tell him anyway.

"Curtis said yes."

"Okay."

"That's it—okay?"

"What do you want me to say? Congratulations, you've scammed your English teacher."

"I just thought you'd want to know."

"So now I know, but I don't get it."

"What don't you get?"

"For starters, why? You've worked your butt off all year to keep a decent grade in honors English and you risk it over a stupid five-page paper? Did you think about what's on that disc?"

"Why are you suddenly so serious about everything? It's one assignment. He might even like it."

"Think, Mitchell. Think about what happens in your movie."

"Our movie."

"No. This is all you. I made a Claymation cartoon that was never supposed to make it out of the troll cave. You cannot blame any of this on me."

CHAPTER 10

Balls, Butts, Puke, and
The Grapes of Wrath

Wallman on the ethics of double dipping:

In the next forty-eight hours, several more people, each in their own way, point out to me that I may not have made the world's most well thought out, reasonable decision.

"You've got balls," Wallman barks at me as David and I enter the film lab after lunch. It isn't immediately apparent whether he's complimenting me or he's upset. David and I both stop in the doorway, unsure of what to do next.

"You turned in the work you did in my class as an assignment for another class. That takes some major balls."

It had never occurred to me. I sort of hadn't remembered that what we did in art counted as an actual class. For one thing, it was fun.

"Well—," David says slowly, thinking this out a little, which is very nice of him considering he isn't the responsible party. I am still in the "oh shit" mode. "Yes, you are right, the same film is being considered as a project for two different teachers, but in very different ways. You, Mr. Wallman, are looking at the technical aspects of the film, its artistic merit, its style and substance. Mr. Curtis is really only considering it as an interpretation of a novel."

"He's a prig and will hate it," Wallman says, laughing behind his beard. "Let me know if he has the guts to fail you." Wallman wanders back toward his desk, stopping to look at some actual digital animation someone has looping on one of the computer screens. I guess the conversation is over. David and I edge our way over to the editing room.

"Do you think Curtis will care that I made the film for another class?"

"He must know. He told Wallman."

I sit down in front of the mixing board. "Thanks for the defense back there. You sounded very convincing."

"For something I was pulling out of my butt. At least Wallman doesn't care."

"Do you really think Curtis will fail me?"

David doesn't answer. He gets out the storyboards for our new project and fiddles with his pencils. He's caught between the need to reassure me as a friend and the urge to tell me one more time what an idiot he thinks I am. I can see the two sides quarreling in his face.

I'm beginning to think that it would have been easier just to read the book.

Carrie on the detrimental effects of pornography on impressionable high school juniors:

"Mitchell, you can't show this."

"Why not?"

"They're naked."

"They're clay."

"They're naked clay."

"It's Adam and Eve. They're supposed to be naked. Anyway, I based it on a painting. The whole point was to have this medieval painting come to life. They aren't really naked, they're nude."

Carrie presses the pause button and points to the screen. "They are naked. You can see Adam's wee-wee." She presses play again. "And there, Eve, full frontal."

Carrie and M.C. had whined the whole way home about why I wouldn't show the movie to them first. So eventually I gave in. Now I remember why "no" was such a better answer.

"I think they're sort of cute," M.C. says. "Except Eve's breasts are a little funny-looking. I think the nipples are too big."

I don't look up at M.C. I know I can't look at her and think the word "nipples" at the same time without getting flustered.

"I think my favorite part," M.C. says, stretching out her feet and resting them on the coffee table, "is when the snake eats Eve and Adam is . . . punished."

"You mean where he is strapped into the giant sewing machine that sews 'sinner' all over his back? I stole it . . . I mean, it's a postmodern reference to a Kafka story. I thought that it was pretty cool. I used a real sewing machine. I don't know why the film lab has one, but it does. Maybe for costumes or sets or something. I cut off a section of his back, placed a few ketchup packets underneath, and then covered over them with clay. I thought the spurting blood was very Tarantino."

"Definitely."

Carrie is less convinced. She fast-forwards and we watch the ketchup packets bursting again. She shakes her head.

"You so jumped the shark."

My mother on parental responsibility:

Eventually David goes home and Carrie and M.C. go off to do whatever it is they spend all their time doing. After verifying that there is not one thing I want to watch on any of the three thousand channels we get, I go look in the kitchen for something to eat. It's almost the same process. There's lots of crap on television, just nothing I want to look at. Our kitchen is full of food, just nothing I want to eat. I don't feel like an apple, grapes, a cheese stick, baby carrots, or leftover roast beef. Actually the roast beef might have been all right, but it's looking a little too left over. There's cans of tuna or soup, but that involves cooking, or at least mixing stuff together. There's peanut butter. In the vegetable drawer there's a few stalks of wilted celery. I decide to make toast.

"Dinner's soon," my mother warns from the living room, where she's on the phone.

"Okay," I tell her. Maybe I'm supposed to stop making toast. But I don't.

I look up from the toaster to find my mother standing in the doorway to the kitchen. She's getting ready to ask me something. It is the preparation-for-confronting-your-child-about-a-difficult-subject face. What did I do now?

I turn to face her. She has wrinkles around her eyes and streaks of gray in her hair, but the twenty-eight years between us doesn't feel as huge as it used to. She's a fund-raising consultant, part-time, and when she is on the phone with a client her voice is assured and invariably cheerful. Friendly but determined; you might like her, but you don't want to get in her way. Lately, at home, her always rightness is less a given, but I don't know whether that's because Carrie and I are getting older or because something about her is changing. Probably some of both.

"Mitch," she says, changing into her smile. Mom often calls me Mitch. I usually object if someone shortens my name, but she named me, so she can get away with it. "Your sister mentioned something about one of your Claymation projects—something you're going to show to your English class."

"Curtis said it was fine. I have his permission."

"Maybe I need to see this . . . thing . . . before you show it in school. Your sister seemed to think it was a bit racy."

"Mom, I'm a junior. Don't you think I'm a little old for you to be checking my homework?"

She considers this. "You're right, I should trust you." I feel a tightness in my chest. That word again.

"I mean, you can see it. I'm not ashamed of it or anything."

"I think I'd like to see it. You already showed it to Carrie."

"That was clearly a mistake. Do you want to see it now?" Do you want to watch it and tell me that there's no way you would let me show this thing in school, then make me read the stupid book and write the paper?

"No, I think I'd like to wait so your dad can watch it too. He's working nights right now, so maybe on a weekend? We'll make some popcorn, have a film festival."

Nothing simple. Can't just watch a movie. Now it's a film festival.

"We could invite your grandmother."

Oh, good.

Chicken—it isn't just for dinner

After dinner, the same Carrie who told me there was no way I could show my film in class declares me chicken-shit for even mentioning the possibility of reading the book. It was just a casual statement like, "You know, maybe I'll try to read *The Grapes of Wrath* after all." Panic had begun to set in. Carrie's point was that if you have decided to screw up your social status, your grade point average, and any hope of ever attending a reasonable four-year university, you might as well have the satisfaction of having done it with conviction. It would seem that I now have some sort of moral obligation to fake it.

I take *The Grapes* to bed with me, but I can't make it past page 23. No matter what is written on the page, the only word that I hear in my head is "nipples."

I really do try not to puke on the carpet

By Thursday, I am past chickenshit and into a full-fledged panic. I wake up in the morning with an honest-to-god stomachache, complete with mild fever and vomiting. Simply nerves, all psychosomatic, but the vomit is real enough and Mom agrees to let me stay home. My dad, who claims to have a medical degree, looks at me lying there and says simply, "Try not to puke on the carpet."

I stay home from school. Mom goes off to work,

Carrie to school, Dad to the hospital. I am now too old for anyone to take time off of work and sit with me for something as minor as a migraine (Dad's conclusion, based on the fact that I have them regularly and they often make me throw up) or the flu (my mother's theory, because it's going around) or being a chickenshit wimp (my sister's more accurate diagnosis). So they leave me sitting up in bed in my bathrobe, with my bedside trash can lined with a plastic bag (just in case), a sick seventeen-year-old who can stay by himself. I may be seventeen, but no one wants to be mature and independent when they feel sick. When you're sick you want someone to fuss over you, make you chickie star soup (Campbell's, from the can), prop you up with pillows, and drag the television in from the playroom.

I don't get up and drag the television in. I don't make myself chickie star soup. In a fit of utter despair and self-loathing, I read the entirety of *The Grapes of Wrath*. Not well, mind you, I'm not that fast a reader, but cover to cover if you don't count eighty or so pages in the middle, which I mostly skip.

"That's pathetic" is Carrie's only comment when she returns at 4:30, M.C. in tow, to discover me on the couch, absorbed in the last chapter.

M.C. is a little more diplomatic. Tossing her backpack onto the ottoman, she finds a perch on one of the green vinyl stools, plucks an apple from the bowl on the counter, and smiles at me. "Did you at least enjoy the book?"

"No. Not really."

"How's your stomach?" asks Carrie, still in the doorway.

"No more puke."

Carrie seems convinced enough to enter the den, but chooses a seat well away from me in case I develop a sudden urge to projectile-vomit across the room. I consider faking it, but I'm afraid it might bring the real thing back up. Carrie eyes me warily. "Are you going to school tomorrow?"

"Yeah. I'm going."

"And . . . ?"

"I think I might write the paper."

"You suck," Carrie declares at my forehead, since I won't lift my face and look her in the eyes. "I can't believe how badly you suck. You're going to chicken out. What a complete wimp. I can't believe you."

Unable to face my sister, I shift my attention to M.C., who is still smiling. She has a piece of green apple skin stuck between her teeth, right next to her left upper canine. I start to tell her, then get embarrassed, and decide instead that it goes well with the freckles on her nose. Something about the freckles and the apple she is chomping on makes me think of Tom Sawyer. M.C. looks out of place in our living room. She should be out convincing someone to whitewash a fence.

I really want to ask her about Curtis, but I don't think

I'm supposed to know and anyway, I'm not sure how I could ask her. I try to imagine her kissing Curtis, but I just can't see it. They don't fit in the same picture. I can imagine M.C. kissing, in fact I can imagine *kissing* M.C., which isn't something I have thought about before—I am suddenly uncomfortable.

M.C. stops chewing for a moment, the half-masticated apple still in her mouth, and shakes her head. The smile never leaves her face. Holding a hand in front of her mouth to block our view of its contents, she declares, "Nope. No paper. You can't write the paper. You have to show the film." Mary Clarissa frequently speaks in pronouncements.

"I don't recall putting you in charge of my life."

"Sorry, but it's true. Can't chicken out now." She returns to chewing happily.

"But I read the book!"

I don't write the essay. It isn't so much that I'm convinced by Carrie and M.C.; I'm just not sure how I would explain to Curtis that I changed my mind. So instead I rip a piece of paper out of my math notebook and jot down all the ways my movie is thematically connected to *The Grapes of Wrath*, in case Curtis challenges me. I come up with four pretty good ones and two more that are kind of a stretch. I don't include Steinbeck as Satan, which would make it seven. I'm back to feeling pretty confident and I start to pick up the phone to call David, which is what

I would normally do, but I don't want to hear him tell me I'm an idiot again. It occurs to me that I always call David. He almost never calls me. Maybe he wouldn't want me to call. I'm still sitting at my desk, phone in hand, ten minutes later when my mother calls me down for dinner.

CHAPTER 11

A Short Dramatic Presentation of a Wells Family Dinner, Followed by a Quick Review of the Entire History of My Love Life

So, dinner

Usual chaos. Conversation of a sort. I imagine conversations the way they appear in books. Orderly paragraphs, properly punctuated. Not in my house.

Carrie and I eat at the breakfast bar, perched on lime-colored vinyl-covered stools that must have been popular in some decade I missed. Mom usually eats standing on the other side of the bar. Tonight she's just standing with her glass of white wine. I always worry a little when Mom isn't eating her own cooking. Maybe she's waiting for Dad, who called and said he would be home in time for dinner. None of us believed him. He's still at work.

Carrie begins:

"Did you buy your prom tickets yet?"

At least it's a new topic. I am not up for another discussion about my English project. While I'm answering that I haven't decided whether or not I'm going, Mom has already jumped in. "Why don't you take M.C.?"

Carrie makes a choking noise, which mirrors my facial reaction.

"Mom, M.C.? I might as well take Carrie."

"Like I'd go with you. Besides, I might have a date."

This is not a surprise. We wait Carrie out for full disclosure. Mom lives for these moments when she gets to hear about our lives. Dinner is banter. It certainly isn't about food, since my mother can barely cook.

"Seth."

"Seth with the trombone or Seth the football player?" I ask.

"Oh, come on." Carrie follows this exclamation with a look that clearly means: "Like I'd date a trombone player."

I chew on my manicotti, which has the consistency of the fruit leather snacks we used to get in our lunchboxes when we were in elementary school. Fruit leather with tomato sauce. I swallow and turn back to Carrie. "You're dating a six-two brainless linebacker?"

"Who's Seth?" Mom asks Carrie.

"He's the tight end . . ."

"You mean he has a tight end," I say.

". . . and he's not brainless."

"He's not brain*ful*."

"So what's wrong with M.C.?" Mom asks, smiling. "She's cute and she's smart."

"Seth is smart too. Don't take Mitchell's side."

"How am I taking Mitchell's side? I don't even know Seth."

"So why is M.C. cute and smart? You are implying that I am interested in Seth just because he's cute."

"And popular."

"Stop it, Mitchell." Carrie glowers at me.

"Mitch, give your sister a break. If she wants to date large, mentally challenged—"

"Mom!"

"So, Mitch, who *are* you going to take to the prom?" Mom asks, taking a sip from her wineglass. It almost sounds like an innocent question. As I begin to repeat that I haven't decided whether I'm going to the prom, Carrie answers for me.

"Amanda."

"Who's Amanda?" asks Mom.

I'm a little too stunned to reply.

Carrie smiles. "This girl in my class who for some inexplicable reason thinks Mitchell is cute. They eat lunch together."

"Twice. We ate lunch twice. You brought her over to the table both times."

Carrie dismisses my comment with a wave of her hand and takes a bite of her manicotti. Mom immediately puts another one on Carrie's plate. You never have an empty plate. You eventually have to leave a little bit or more food will appear. Mom, despite an advanced degree, never seems to recognize the meaning of "No, thank you, I've had enough."

I look down at my half-eaten dinner. Manicotti are really just penne on hormones.

"Anyway," Carrie continues, "she'll go with you. She and I are prom dress shopping Saturday."

"She sounds very nice," Mom says. "She should come for dinner."

"How do you know she'll go with me? I haven't asked her. I haven't even thought of asking her." I am feeling somewhat irrelevant to the process.

"I asked her for you," Carrie explains. "She said yes. You still should call her about it, though."

I'm now at a loss for words, so Mom jumps right back in. "So, who's M.C. going with?"

"David."

"Does he know?" I ask.

"There's no reason for sarcasm, Mitch. Your sister makes a wonderful social director. You guys certainly aren't doing much about it on your own. Besides, I think David's sweet on M.C." I happen to know that David is not sweet on M.C., but I'm not sure how to explain it. I'm just relieved she's not planning on going with Curtis. Mom, however, is on a roll. "We could have dinner for you here. I could make a special meal and appetizers, maybe a little champagne. We could decorate the dining room really formally . . ."

"Mom, we are not having the prom dinner at our house. They serve dinner at the prom."

"Not this year," says Carrie.

"What's not this year?" Mom asks.

"No dinner. The dance committee is full of these prom princesses who don't think hotel catering is good enough. Seth already has reservations at the Ratcliffe House."

"Nice," Mom says, then turns toward me. "So where will you and David take Amanda and M.C.?"

"I don't know. Ask Carrie."

Carrie doesn't miss a beat. "Georgio's."

I almost choke on my manicotti. Mom gives a low whistle. "Wow. That's a really . . ."

"Expensive," I stammer.

". . . nice, nice restaurant. You must like this Amanda girl a lot," she says without sarcasm.

A short history of my entire love life

Just for the record, since we are talking about proms, I should point out that I am the single biggest loser on the face of the planet. Not that I think anybody needs convincing, but I would like to offer the following as evidence. I am seventeen years old and my entire romantic life has consisted of:

1) Kissing exactly two females who are unrelated to me
2) Having been on one date

I should probably admit that the two kisses occurred at a party in seventh grade. The two females in question kissed practically everyone at the party. It was some sort of dare thing. My active involvement was basically happening to stand in the right room. Given the speed of the lip action, I was lucky to escape unbruised.

The one date was with Mariel. We went to a dance together in eighth grade. She asked me. Her mother drove. She danced with her friends. I stood near the water fountain.

I feel like I've been standing by that same water fountain now for the last four years.

CHAPTER 12

Showtime

Drum roll, please

I'm not sure what I expected to happen. We get to class and there's a TV with a DVD player on a rolling cart at the front of the room. Curtis has obviously thought ahead and requested it. He asks whether I want to go first or wait until the end of class. All I want to do is go, go away, disappear, but I agree to show my film first because the alternative, sitting there thinking about it through the whole class, seems unbearable.

It takes a little longer than usual for everyone to get settled. Some of the chairs have to be rearranged so that everyone can see the screen, and there's a little futzing with the DVD player, because it isn't actually connected to the TV, but eventually everyone has a seat and the equipment is attached. Curtis spends a few minutes reminding everyone who hasn't turned in a paper yet about the penalties for late assignments, then gives a shortened version of his monthly lecture on the privileges and responsibilities inherent in this being an honors class. And then he turns to me.

"Mr. Wells"—Curtis never refers to us by our first names—"will now grace us with his latest feature film, a blockbuster titled . . ." He pauses and looks at me.

" 'An Animated Exploration of Biblical Themes in John Steinbeck's *The Grapes of Wrath*,' " I mumble.

There are a few disapproving grumbles, but Curtis smiles. "It sounds quite exciting."

Quite exciting. "Quite" may be my least favorite adverb. There are more groans from the class, but they are mostly good-natured. Whatever this film is, it has to be better than listening to Curtis drone on.

"Is there something you wish to say by way of an introduction?" prompts Curtis.

"No," I think, "I want to die and puke. Or maybe puke, then die." Instead I stand up, turn to face the class, and say, "This is a Claymation film I made as my report." I sit back down.

"Afterward, you will, no doubt, entertain questions." He seems quite amused. *Quite.* He is enjoying something about this situation. At first I think it's just my embarrassment, but it occurs to me suddenly that this might be Curtis's way of trying to be warm and friendly. I don't want to think of Curtis as warm and friendly.

"Sure," I mumble, not at all sure.

"Then proceed," Curtis commands, and I slide the disc into the slot on the player, press play, and sit down.

Someone has left the sound set on the highest level, and the distorted cacophony of the opening theme blaring through the tiny monitor speakers makes everyone jump. Everyone except Curtis, who calmly picks up the remote and resets the volume to a reasonable level.

The next seven minutes are excruciating. In slow motion every mistake leaps off the screen at me: the jumpy editing, Wallman's voice shouting across the lab during one of the voiceovers, the fingers holding the disco-dancing Satan (a naked Ken doll with a picture of Steinbeck's face taped to it). It all seems so amateurish, so horribly, sincerely, sophomorically dumb.

It is hard to tell if anyone else notices. There are a few guffaws, mostly during the nude scene, and one "cool" in a particularly bloody sequence. No one falls asleep. Mariel takes notes. When it's finally over, I stand up, push the eject button, and take out my DVD, all without daring to look at anyone. I am on my way back to my seat when Curtis clears his throat and motions me back to the front of the room.

"Don't forget questions." He is still smiling.

No one has questions.

There is an awkward silence while I consider whether it's possible to transfer schools in the second semester of one's junior year. It is possibly the longest stretch of silence I have ever experienced in Curtis's class.

"Perhaps you might say a little about how you make this kind of film. It was really quite inventive."

So I explain. Yes, it is in monotone without looking anyone in the eye and no, I don't raise my voice above a whisper, but I give a reasonably detailed account of how a Claymation film is made. I describe the storyboards and the editing, the ketchup packets, and how the live action and the stop action work together. I tell them about my favorite Claymation animators and which parts of this film were influenced by Nick Park and suddenly we can hear the sounds of lockers slamming and people in the hallway. Class is over.

Thunderous applause, sort of

I look up, startled.

"Excellent," Curtis says brightly over the noise of everyone packing up their backpacks and filing out. "Monday we will continue with Willa Cather. It's on the syllabus." He is practically ebullient. "Nice job, Mr. Wells," he says, turning to me.

"Thanks. I'm glad you liked it?" It isn't meant to be a question, but it comes out that way anyway.

"Interesting, creative, well executed."

"Thanks," I mutter again, picking up my backpack. I feel it might be rude if I run to the door, so I just sort of edge my way out. Curtis keeps on smiling. He suddenly seems as uncomfortable as I am. Maybe he doesn't have anything else to say. I have a flash of awareness where I can imagine that he might wonder later whether he said the right thing in response to me.

There is no sudden outpouring of reaction from my classmates. In fact, no one makes a single comment except Louis, who says something like "Eve had nice tits" loud enough for me to hear, but not directly to me and probably not for my benefit. Danielle sort of smiles at me on the way out, but I think that's mostly because I'm in her way. Her eye shadow is blue.

David is waiting in the hallway.

Define "great"

"Was it okay?" I ask him.

"It went great," he tells me, nodding but not elaborating. "Great."

David's reassurance is not reassuring. He is my friend. He helped make this thing. And although the word "great" sounds positive, it was not said with any conviction.

"Are you angry because he liked it?" I ask, trying not to sound defensive.

"I'm not angry."

"I don't mean *angry* angry. Just a little angry because you were wrong."

"I'm not angry."

"What are you?"

"Almost late for history. Other than that—not much. What's up your ass?" David's tone is even, but to me it still sounds aggressive.

"Nothing. At least it's over," I say, more to myself than to him, as we find our regular seats in history.

The rest of the day is pretty much unbearable. I don't want to sit through history, or chemistry. Chemistry last period Friday is almost inhuman to begin with. Today it is a visit to the orthodontist, dinner in a fancy restaurant with my aunt Norma, and that documentary on making pencils we had to watch in fourth grade, all compacted into forty-five minutes. I had no idea that so much boredom could be crammed into less than an hour.

Nevertheless, I dread going home. I was thinking David and I would go out and do something to celebrate or at least go do something, but he went to practice without his usual one-word invitations (movie? pizza? party?) and I'm not calling. Plus, I know my mother will not let this kind of event go unacknowledged. I expect her to meet me at the door with a bouquet of flowers or something, so her shouted "How'd it go?" from the kitchen catches me off guard.

"Standing O?" she asks.

"No one threw vegetables."

"There go our dinner plans. Did Mr. Curtis say anything?"

"No, not really. He seemed okay about it."

"Tea?"

"Okay."

I don't really want tea, but I don't feel like going to my room and dealing with my life either. My mother would desperately like to have children who would sit with her every afternoon and tell her all about their lives. Instead, sometimes we have tea. I pour the water into two mugs and choose what seems to me the least offensive of the thirty-five or so flavors of herbal tea we keep in a big jar on the counter. I can't deal with any of the berry flavors, teas with names that don't indicate contents (Sleepy-time, Peppy), or anything labeled "zinger." I stick with simple, easily identifiable flavors: peppermint, chamomile, vanilla. I settle on chamomile.

"You seem a little let down," she offers.

No comment seems necessary, so instead I scald my tongue on my tea.

Mom sits and looks at me expectantly. This is supposed to be a moment, a child-parent poignant memory: the two of us sitting in the kitchen drinking tea after a bad day, talking, communicating, sharing. She is trying so hard to be there for me that I almost try to tell her what is going on, but I can't, or won't. So we do what we normally do; she asks me questions and I give her content. The fact is I'm not sure why I feel so let down. It all went well, but I'm almost in tears when I tell her that chemistry was totally boring, and I'm thinking of blue eye shadow when I describe my little impromptu speech on the art of Claymation. And no, I'm not doing anything tonight, there's a party but I don't think David's going and I don't feel like going by myself. And, as the conversation shifts, it's fine that we aren't going skiing, I have a history project due on Monday, and no, no, no, I'm not making another film.

CHAPTER 13

Missing—One English Teacher, Last Seen Wearing a Tie and Carrying a Really Boring Novel

At least we noticed he left

My film having received its debut, English class is off to new topics. I don't ask about my grade for the project. Papers will be returned on Wednesday and I assume whatever comments Curtis is going to give me about my film will arrive on Wednesday with the rest. Curtis always returns papers exactly one week after they are turned in. He seems to think that he has some sort of moral responsibility to be consistent and timely.

As I sit in class mentally calculating how many more hours of Curtis's lecturing I still have to endure—less than fifty, if I'm doing the math correctly—I begin to sense that something is wrong. Curtis is talking, nothing unusual there, but his voice seems flatter, less animated, as if he no longer cares about whether or not we are listening. He is almost mumbling, reading aloud occasionally from his well-worn copy of *O Pioneers!* sitting on his stool at the front of the room, which is unusual in itself, as he usually paces while he reads. The board is nearly blank. Last Friday's date still sits in the far left corner. There are a few half-hearted attempts to write a word or two, none of the usual illegible scrawl he haphazardly fills the board with as he writes furiously with one hand, holding the book in the other and never stopping the rush of words for so much as a breath. Today there are pauses. He has not asked one rhetorical question. In fact, he has asked no questions at all.

I look around furtively to see if anyone else has noticed the change. If anyone has, it is hard to tell. Several people are still taking notes, on Lord knows what, because Curtis has barely said anything about the reading. The same one or two students who always sleep through the class have their heads down in their customary hunched positions. The rest of the class sit in their usual semi-dazed state.

The pauses grow longer. Curtis reads, then pauses, says a few words, then pauses again, as if he is testing whether there is a difference between the pauses and the talking. And then, unostentatiously, he closes the book and walks out of the room.

At first, no one speaks. The heads that are down on the desktops remain there; the more alert students look around nervously. Mariel stops taking notes.

"Maybe he needs to take a leak," suggests Louis. No one laughs.

We sit in silence for over a minute. I time it on my watch. Then Bonnie and Anna, who sit in the far side back corner, start to whisper, pulling their desks closer together. Slowly small clumps of conversation sprout across the room, and eventually people find their normal speaking voices. David doesn't move from his spot, third row, third seat in, and he becomes an island as the neat lines of desks form loose constellations of social organization. He fidgets with his pencils. I pretend to be part of the conversation taking place directly to my left, about a movie I hadn't seen. My one contribution is that I had heard it was good. At 9:05, when class officially ends, everyone gets up and leaves.

"What was the last thing he said?" I ask David as we shuffle down the hallway to calculus.

"I wasn't really listening," David admits with what sounds like regret.

"I don't think anyone was."

"Should we tell someone?"

"Report Curtis AWOL? I don't want to get him in trouble. Maybe he had a breakdown, like Ms.—what was the name of the woman who we had in seventh-grade Latin?"

"Ms. Hertig."

"Like Ms. Hertig."

David shakes his head. "She started out weirder than Curtis. Curtis is strange, but not psycho. And she didn't walk out of class, she broke into hysterics and threw a chair at Louis."

Theory 1: A man walks into a bar . . .

Mariel, of course, has the full story by break.

"He just walked out of school, got in his car, and drove away. They found his copy of *O Pioneers!* in the parking lot."

"Does anybody know why?"

Mariel grins. "It's a mystery, but the prevailing theory is that some trustee spotted Curtis coming out of Riley's."

Riley's is the best-known, and possibly only, gay bar in town.

"They can't fire a guy for going into a bar, not even Riley's."

"Even if it was on a school night," adds David.

"Was that a joke?" Mariel asks. "I could have sworn you lacked the gene for sarcasm."

David almost smiles. "I never joke," he replies solemnly.

Mariel spots someone else she needs to tell the story to and walks away. I have to ask David.

"Do you really think Curtis is gay?"

He readjusts his glasses, a clear signal that he's annoyed. "Why would I know?"

◉　◎　◎

On Tuesday, we have a substitute English teacher who clearly has not read *O Pioneers!* and tries to engage us in a

94

discussion of William Catheter's work. She isn't much older than we are. My guess is that she was student-teaching somewhere and got shuffled into this slot at the last minute. She seems intimidated. This is new to us. Honors English classes are rarely seen as frightening.

"I'm an early childhood specialist," she confesses about halfway through the period in a desperate attempt to elicit some sympathetic response. Her styled hair, manicured nails, and short tight skirt are, however, more interesting than anything she has to say. The sub has pulled one of the student desks forward to face the class, and she keeps tugging at that skirt as if it might suddenly grow larger, which would have been useful, as it barely covers her thighs. Every time she shifts her legs, she offers glimpses of her pale blue panties. I don't think I'm the only one who notices this. Several males in the classroom seem unusually attentive.

On Wednesday, Ms. Blue Panties has mysteriously disappeared, replaced by a youngish bearded guy wearing a tie and Vans. It is as if they're sending us stereotypes of bad teachers. Every other sentence ends with a rhetorical "Right?" Example: "Cather is really challenging our preconceived notions of femininity, right?" I have visions of the class chanting "Right!" in response, amen-style, but of course no one says anything. After seventeen or eighteen rhetorical "rights?" the sub finally asks, "Has anyone read any of this?" No one answers. The few who have actually done the assigned reading aren't about to admit to it. He looks disappointed, then brightens up. "So what music do you guys listen to? Anybody into Animal Collective?"

I am beginning to miss Curtis.

On Thursday, I am summoned to the principal's office.

Saying I was summoned to the Director of the Upper Division's office just doesn't have the same ring

I have never been in trouble before. I can't remember ever even being sent to sit in the hall, or having a teacher raise their voice at me. This is my fourteenth year at Richard White Day School; I started in preK. Thirteen and a half years of reasonably good behavior. I don't know how to react.

We don't actually have a principal—at least not by that title. Some consultant had been hired two years ago to reorganize Richard White Day to reflect the reality of the business climate of small expensive private schools, and now everyone has pseudo-corporate titles that look nice on their business cards. There are no deans or headmasters in this progressive institution. Instead, we have a CEO, Dr. VandeNeer, whom we see at assemblies twice a year and on brochures. His primary job seems to be schmoozing with donors and bringing in the bucks. He must be doing pretty well since every room, every hallway, even some of the larger windows have neat little plaques with someone's name on them. I often drink from the J. P. Gilley water fountain, which happens to be near my locker. Louis suggested giving a new urinal as our class gift so we could have a plaque in the john.

The business manager has become a CFO (Chief Financial Officer), although everybody still calls him the BM, just not to his face. Most of the other administrators have become directors: Director of the Lower Grades, Director of the Middle Grades, Directors of Admissions, Publications, Academic Computing, Media Center, and even Student Services (formerly the janitors and kitchen crew). Teachers are still teachers and, as far as I know, we are still officially designated students, not yet products in need of bar coding.

So I'm not summoned to the principal's office. I am summoned to the Director of the Upper Division's office. We call him Mr. Sorrelson.

Mr. Sorrelson is nice enough most of the time, but he has a reputation for losing his temper easily and having an intimidating presence. I come in already intimidated. He is in his early fifties and was brought to White Day when the board decided that the former headmaster had been too liberal and, well . . . nice. We needed more discipline or something, and Sorrelson was supposed to be a hard-ass. He plays the role pretty well. He has a large head with scattered white strands of hair on top and a droopy chin below. The rest of him isn't as large, except for his belly, which protrudes forward like he's very pregnant. His lower lip sticks out when he's riled, his jaw set in an angry grimace. His lip is out when I enter the room.

Mr. Sorrelson sits behind an imposing wooden desk that almost entirely fills his tiny office. Lord knows how they got the thing in there. Since there isn't enough room to place it on the far wall, the desk faces the adjacent wall. As a consequence, to anyone passing by, Sorrelson is always in profile. The desk is immaculate, no spare paper clips, no loose papers, only a small three-tiered plastic in-box and a telephone on three yards of brightly polished wood. Two small plastic chairs are wedged in between the far side of the desk and the wall.

"Please sit down, Mitchell," Mr. Sorrelson barks. Barking "please" is one of the things that make people like Mr. Sorrelson seem intimidating. I sit down.

"Do you know why I have asked you to come to my office?"

I want to answer, "No, don't you?" but I don't. I hate this question. Maybe he is hoping I'll admit to doing something he doesn't know about yet, like drug-dealing or beating up freshmen or something.

"No," I finally say.

Mr. Sorrelson tugs on his lower lip thoughtfully, as if

he is still deciding what it is that I have done. I can feel the blood rushing in my ears, that odd pseudo-heartbeat you get when you're nervous. I'm nervous.

"Correct me if I'm wrong, but I believe you turned in a video, a cartoon or something, for your last English project." It takes him a good ten seconds to get this line out. He clears his throat twice and makes odd clicking noises with his tongue as he speaks, as if there is too much moisture in his mouth. It comes out more like "Correct (uhem) me (slurp) if I'm (ich) wrong (uhem), but (ich) I be (ych) lieve (sluurrll)." At least he doesn't drool. I can only imagine that he considers this long drawn-out method of communicating a nifty way of heightening the tension.

"Yeah."

"And I suppose you thought that this little cartoon of yours was funny. A real joke."

I nod. I did. "Parts of it were intended to be humorous," I suggest somewhat lamely. "It was supposed to be a visual interpretation of biblical themes in Steinbeck's *Grapes of Wrath*."

"I know who wrote *The Grapes of Wrath*," Sorrelson intones, as if he had caught Steinbeck earlier and already punished him for it. He stares at me, knitting his unruly white eyebrows together. "Had it occurred to you at any point in this process that someone might find this little cartoon of yours . . ." He pauses and looks at the ceiling for a moment, as if he needs to summon the next word from above, and then with sudden fury he discovers it among the fluorescent lights and, lowering his gaze, he spits it at me: ". . . *offensive?!?!*"

I panic. "No. I mean, I knew that there was a little nudity, but it isn't very explicit and they are made out of clay, I mean they don't look like people, they look more like those little Fisher-Price figures, except Eve has breasts but you wouldn't know they were breasts except that they're round and where breasts should be, but if they weren't there you would think that they were . . . little tiny half-grapefruits or something, but really tiny, so I didn't think anyone would be too upset by little toylike naked clay things, oh, except for the dancing Steinbeck, which is a naked Ken doll, but they aren't anatomically correct anyway . . ." I run out of steam. Mr. Sorrelson is staring at me quizzically.

"There was nudity? No one said anything about nudity."

Crap.

"Well," continues Mr. Sorrelson, who now seems a bit flustered, which has the advantage of making him talk more quickly. "The issue wasn't about the nudity, but we'll come back to that later. I have received several complaints from quite a few families . . ."

There is something in the way he says "quite a few" that makes me question the claim. How many people need to call to constitute "quite a few"?

Sorrelson takes a deep breath and continues in a tone that almost sounds confidential. "We had a few calls saying that your cartoon was a parody of the Bible and was inappropriate to show to a class that includes people of deep religious conviction."

"Oh."

"Was that your intention?"

"To make fun of somebody's religion? No."

"Do you see how someone might interpret your cartoon this way?"

"Maybe." I'm biting the inside of my lip and thinking through the sequences. You'd have to be pretty damn sensitive.

"I think the best thing would be for you to bring the DVD in and let me watch it, and we will continue from there. In the meantime, I will call your parents and inform them of our discussion today. I assume that they have seen your cartoon." He is back to talking slowly.

I shake my head.

"Perhaps you may wish to show it to them before you bring it to me. Do you have anything else to say?"

I shake my head again.

"Then you may return to your class."

"Thanks," I say, although I'm not sure why I'm thanking him for this unpleasant experience.

Mom loves the film. Dad, who actually likes Steinbeck, thinks it's a bit harsh, but makes several encouraging comments about technical features, such as the melting figures in the dust bowl and the flying monkey sequence. Carrie tells me that it's better the second time, but it's still gross. We eat popcorn. I can't imagine this is what Mr. Sorrelson had envisioned when he told me to show the "cartoon" to my parents.

CHAPTER 14

Oncoming Trains and a
Large Variety of Similarly Strained
Metaphors

Butterflies, bondage, and balloons

I miss David," Carrie says as she stands with me and M.C. waiting for Mom to pick us up.

"You miss his car."

Baseball season is in full swing. David has retrieved his glove from underneath his mattress, where it had hibernated all winter wrapped around a baseball. It was a little like watching a butterfly emerge from its chrysalis, only a lot less picturesque. Suddenly there were lots of very important conversations he had to have with teammates he'd barely spoken to in the off-season. And suddenly our designated chauffeur became much less available.

Sometimes I drive when Mom doesn't need the car. Other times we have to wait for Mom to pick us up. Mom is always late, so not only do we not get to drive ourselves home, but we have to stand around watching everyone else leave, knowing that when they look out the window of their various sports utility vehicles and occasional second-hand wrecks they see supposed high school students pathetically waiting for their mommy to pick them up. For Carrie, it is slow torture, even worse than having to ride home with me in the minivan.

"Do you think," M.C. says, staring out at the pond, "that when we're old, we'll remember anything about high school? How much does it matter? As long as we make it to college, will anything that's happening now even be important to us in ten years?"

"How long is baseball season?" Carrie asks.

"All spring," I answer.

M.C. is in melancholy. Maybe she's missing Curtis. "You know," she says in a low monotone, "everything we care about now—grades, hair, boys—when we leave here, we won't give a crap about any of it."

"I'll still care about my hair," Carrie says. "And boys will be men then and we'll probably care about them about as much as we do now."

"But differently, you know?"

The three of us are now the only ones left in the pickup area. Carrie is pacing the road. I give up and go sit on one of the benches. It may be baseball season, but it's unseasonably chilly. I dig my hands into my jacket pockets.

M.C. sits next to me and we don't say anything for way too long. I am in my own funk. This morning I dropped off my movie with Sorrelson's administrative assistant, who gave me the kind of thin smile you give someone who you don't quite trust but are trying to placate into going away as quickly as possible. She held the sides of the case as if it were contaminated and said a simple "Thank you" in response. I waited for too long thinking I was supposed to receive some sort of instructions, but she just repeated "Thank you" and smiled again, and I left. I'm assuming Sorrelson will let me know my fate sometime soon. I feel like one of those cartoon heroines tied to a track watching a very slow train coming to run me over. A very, very slow train.

"What are you thinking?" I ask M.C.

"Ice cream."

"It's freezing."

"We don't have to eat it outside."

"But in ten years . . ."

"I'll still want ice cream."

We convince Mom to let us drop her off at home, and the three of us go out to the mall for ice cream. I know I'm transportation, not company, but M.C. has cheered up and Carrie's not being any more obnoxious than usual.

M.C. orders a banana split with everything. I have one scoop of chocolate ice cream with pineapple topping. Carrie orders a Diet Coke.

I have never seen anyone devour a banana split the way that M.C. does. If we came here to change her mood, it's worked. M.C. is a frenzy of eating. She digs straight into the middle, where the chocolate sauce is melting into the ice cream and pulls large spoonfuls out, slurping them down with gleeful abandon. She picks up the banana slices with her fingers, leaving a trail of drips on the table, on her shirt, on her chin. She has ice cream in her hair. She unself-consciously licks the splattered whipped cream off the back of her hand and smiles at me.

"Don't you love banana splits?"

The door of the restaurant opens. Carrie looks up and then away, pretending that she didn't see who came in. Ryan, Danielle, Nicole, and some guy I don't know are standing at the door. M.C. turns around in her chair to see who Carrie is so carefully ignoring and all of her happy energy drains away. It's like watching a balloon deflate. She spins back around and grabs a napkin. As the foursome walks past us to find a table, we sit absolutely silent, as if maybe we are invisible and if we don't say anything they won't notice we are here. Of the four, only Danielle seems a little awkward about completely snubbing us; she gives us a little "Hi guys," and a wave. "Hi," I answer, and maybe there's a nod from Ryan. They settle into a table on the other side of a line of booths.

"What?" I ask Carrie.

"It's a guy M.C. knows."

"*That* guy?"

"Yes?" Carrie answers.

"Knows?"

"Knew."

"Can we go?" M.C. asks.

Louis explains the wedgie inquisition

"Are we going to the prom?"

"Together?" David asks me. I think he means it as a joke.

"Carrie wants to set me up with Amanda."

David doesn't answer immediately. He lays out his napkin, arranges his lunch, and opens his chips. Maybe he's thinking. I look at his sandwich.

"Turkey? It's been ham for three days and now suddenly turkey? You never switch mid-week."

"What do you have today? You are always obnoxious about my lunch when yours sucks."

I look in my bag. There is a thermos of something. Thermoses are almost always a bad sign.

"You know, I don't think you like turkey that much. And you don't look hungry. Now that it's baseball season, you've really got to watch your weight. And a whole sandwich?"

David hands me half of his sandwich. "I should just start packing two."

"Bert, Ernie, how's funny?" Louis pulls a chair from a neighboring table and places it directly next to mine. He reaches over me, removes the sandwich from David's hand, takes a large bite of it, and then gives it back. Chewing and grinning and shaking his head at the same time, he turns back toward me.

"So, Spielberg, rumors are that Sorrelson gave your effort a thumbs-down. Rotten tomatoes. No stars."

David is looking at the remains of his sandwich, trying to figure out how he feels about eating it after Louis's bite. He decides against it and places it back onto his napkin. Louis picks it up and finishes it in two large chomps.

"You're not so used to being hauled in by the inquisition, are you? Prissy boys like you guys who spend all their time calculating their GPAs to the fifth decimal point don't do the heart-to-hearts with the drool king often. Hung you by your wedgie, didn't he? How are those balls feeling these days? A little squeezed?"

"I don't think it's a big deal," I say, with no confidence in my voice.

"Probably not. Just your future. Any chance of success later in life. That permanent record has legs, you know. It gets up and follows you everywhere you go. 'Mitchell Wells, we were going to offer you the vice presidency of our gigantic corporation, but I see here that your high school principal says you're a bad apple.' 'Dr. Wells, I'm afraid we will have to reject your license on ethical grounds. We see in this file that you are a pornographer and blasphemer.' On the plus side, you can probably convince some floozy to marry you. Guys with reps, you know, always in demand."

He leans in closer to me. "Don't let them get to you. They've got nothing, no leverage at all. Sorrelson, that belly of his is full of hot air and he makes those faces at you"— Louis sticks out his lower lip and frowns—"but what's he really going to do? Tell your mommy? Make you sit in the library for a day suffering the horrors of missing Ms. Bexter sighing her way through math class? Sorrelson can't do squat and he knows it." Still only inches away from my face, he bellows in a suddenly deep voice, "Pay no attention to the man behind the curtain!"

With that, he stands up, palms David's apple, and strides out of the cafeteria.

"What's in the thermos?" David asks.

I hand it over and he opens it, grimaces, and hands it back.

"Maybe I'll buy something." He looks around, distracted. "You didn't tell me you had to go talk to Sorrelson," he says to the empty chair next to him.

"It was a couple of days ago. He asked me to bring the film in, but he hasn't gotten back to me about it."

"Are you in trouble?"

"I don't know yet. Someone complained that it was offensive." I shrug like it's all no big deal.

"How come you didn't tell me?"

I don't know. I was going to tell him right after it happened, but we weren't ever alone in the hallway and then he went to practice. And then on Friday I was going to bring it up at lunch, but we spent the whole period talking about something else. And then it was the weekend and we went to a movie but we didn't really talk, and now it is Monday, and it felt weird to bring it up since it happened four days ago.

"I guess because nothing's happened yet," I lie.

"Could you e-mail or something if you get expelled? Just to keep me in the loop."

"I'll send you an invite to the hanging. I know how you feel about missing big social events."

"Gay" as a metaphor for everything that's fucked up between us

There is a moment a few hours later when we almost communicate. We are standing next to each other in the hallway outside the film lab. The trolls are inside, the previous class is long gone, and David asks what's wrong with me lately.

"I don't know how to act around you anymore," I answer.

"Since when?"

"Since you told me."

"Oh," David says.

"I mean, I don't think you want me to act any different. Differently."

"Does it make you nervous that I'm . . ."

"Gay?" I need to say it.

"Does it?"

"Maybe."

"Are you afraid someone will find out and think you are too?"

"No."

"Are you afraid I'm going to try to kiss you, or feel you up or something?"

"No—of course not."

David takes two steps forward and looks me square in the face. I can't read him at all. He doesn't look angry. Is he hoping that I'll lean over and kiss him? Is that what he wants?

I turn my head and stare at a spot several feet to my left.

"I'm just afraid I'll say the wrong thing." My voice comes out quiet, almost believable. I don't look up for David's reaction.

We stand there. Months, maybe years go by and we don't say a word. Then we go into class.

CHAPTER 15

You Know, Guy Stuff

Thud

We go watch David play baseball. Actually, we go watch David watch baseball, since he hasn't seen a minute of action all season. Making varsity doesn't mean that you play varsity.

We constitute a small crowd all by ourselves. Carrie and M.C. are here. So is Amanda. And my mother. Mom is here because Mom is a baseball fan. Mention baseball and she becomes another person. She cares deeply about who is on top in the American League. She always has an opinion on trades and salaries and which records require asterisks. She and David can sit happily in the kitchen arguing about who should have gotten the Cy Young and whether the Mets will suck again this year. Her own children, who have never showed any interest in the all-American pastime, are a disappointment to her.

So Mom is at the game, perched in the stands wearing

her Red Sox hat with a small ponytail sticking out the back. She gives a little wave to David, who smiles but does not wave back. His parents won't be here. He has told them not to come and they will be more than happy to oblige. He does not look up at me.

Although there were four of us in the minivan, I am the only one sitting with Mom. I wonder if I should be more self-conscious about sitting in the stands with my mother, but I don't really have much choice. Carrie would probably prefer a tonsillectomy to sitting near Mom at a baseball game. Between Mom's baseball cap and her regular, often vulgar taunting of the umpire, I can understand Carrie's embarrassment. But my mother would be offended if I left her by herself. I also don't have anyone else to sit with. As long as she doesn't hold my hand when she gets excited, which she has been known to do, I will sit with her. But I am not willing to hold hands with my mother in public.

Carrie is not a baseball fan. She's here mostly to scope out the players. I suspect that Amanda and M.C.'s presence is part of Carrie's prom strategy. Of the three of them, only M.C. looks like she is focused on baseball. She is sort of squinting at the field as if something is written on it explaining what is going on. Every once in a while she will clap, sometimes even at the right time. Mom whoops when we score on a well-hit double in the third inning. Following her lead, M.C. gives a little "Go Blue!"

cry, but it isn't convincing. I'm pretty sure she has no idea what she's watching.

I steal a glance at Amanda, who is sitting quietly beside Carrie, and I catch her eye by mistake. She smiles at me. I turn my attention back to the game in panic. We score another run and David stands up in the dugout to give a whistle and clap. High fives all around, as Glenn takes off his helmet and sits down. David may not be playing, but he looks right in his uniform. His blond hair sticks out from under his cap, framing his face. The shirt hangs well from his shoulders—he must be lifting weights. If he could ditch his glasses, he could be in a beer commercial. I try to imagine him through the eyes of the trio of females watching him from the stands. He's good-looking. I bet M.C. would think he has a nice butt.

At the top of the sixth, with one out, runners on second and third, the cleanup batter for the other team hits a hard line drive to our shortstop, who stops it short. Unable to decide whether to throw to first for the out or to the catcher to hold the runner on third, he instead hurls the ball straight into the home team dugout. I'm thinking error. I'm not sure whether David was attempting to catch it or just trying to get out of the way, but he half stands up, which puts him directly into the ball's flight path. There is a very loud thud, and now everyone is standing to watch David topple over the bench backward, taking the rest of the second string with him.

"I think he got it in the head," Mom says, and she runs down the steps of the bleachers toward the dugout. Maybe she feels responsible for David as a surrogate parent. Maybe she just wants to see what happened. Three rounds of deciding I should go too and then deciding that I shouldn't, I decide I should and I follow my mother. She has a good lead on me, and by the time I get to the dugout she is talking to the trainer, who holds an icepack on David's head.

"He's fine, sweetie," Mom tells me.

"It was just his head," the trainer says, deadpan. "He wasn't using it much anyway. Although this may be a first for me."

"What is?" asks David, who is now holding the icepack himself and looks a little firmer.

"I'm not sure we've had anyone who's managed to get injured while sitting on the bench. Usually you have to be in the game."

No, no, no, yes, yes

Mom won't let David drive home in case he has a concussion or something. As a responsible parent, she decides to drive him home in his car so she can let his parents know what happened. I am instructed to take Amanda, Carrie, and M.C. home. Amanda didn't come with us, so I am a little suspicious about why I now need to give her a ride. Still, how much of a setup can this be? She didn't bean David with a ball, and Carrie and M.C. are in the car with us. Carrie and M.C. race to the car to take the backseat and ensure Amanda rides shotgun. They aren't very subtle.

Amanda's idea of conversation is to ask lots of questions. It feels a little like an interrogation.

"Do you go to all the home games?"

"No."

"Do you play baseball?"

"No."

"Are you a Braves fan?"

"No."

Without looking in the rearview mirror, I can tell that Carrie is groaning and rolling her eyes. She is so embarrassed by me.

Amanda goes to a lot of games, plays softball, and loves the Braves.

"Do you think David has a concussion?"

"No."

"That must have really hurt, don't you think?"

"Yes."

"Is David your best friend?"

"Yes."

Amanda thinks it was probably just a bruise, but it does hurt and she knows because she once got walloped by a field hockey ball. Did I know she played field hockey too?

She grills me about what teachers I have for what subjects. My taste in music. Whether I've ever played a musical instrument. She's played cello since she was six. It is a long ride home.

Oh, yeah. Oops.

Dad meets us at the door, looking for dinner. Dad can cook, but you have to tell him that he's supposed to or it just doesn't happen. If he hadn't married Mom while he was still in residency, he might have starved. Carrie shows him where the kitchen is and reminds him how to boil pasta. We are searching for something to put on it when the phone rings.

"Oh, yeah. Oops," Carrie says. "I'll tell him. Hey, Mitchell, forget something?"

I can't think of anything.

"Do you want to go back and pick up our mother? We stranded her at David's house."

Oh, yeah. Oops.

On the way home my mother tells me how worried she is about David. I listen carefully, because when she is worried about me she often expresses it in terms of her anxiety about David.

"I think he's too shy."

David's not shy. No one would call him gregarious, but he's not shy.

"About girls."

Oh.

"Has he asked M.C. to the prom yet?"

No. But I don't know if anyone has told him he's supposed to. I certainly haven't. Mom has been focused on the prom lately, partly because Carrie is obsessed with it and partly because she thinks it is a good opportunity for David and me to go out with girls.

"We haven't talked about the prom," I tell her.

"What do you guys talk about?"

"Explosives, red meat, professional wrestling. You know, guy stuff."

Normal

David has decided that we need to be more normal. That's what he says when he calls me. His head is just fine, we need to be normal, and he will be by to pick me up at 8:13. It's a Monday, but I don't argue. When he pulls up at 8:11, I ask where we are going and get a "just get in the car," and so I do. He drives about a quarter of a mile from my house into what might be a future cul-de-sac. This end of the development is still being built; there are no houses on this little road, just a few large piles of dirt and some scrap wood that someone dumped here. It isn't scenic, but it's deserted. It occurs to me that this is the kind of place where you'd expect to find some couple parked making out.

"We are seventeen years old. We should be drinking

more." David reaches behind the front seat and produces a brown paper bag. We get out of the car and sit on the curb. David pulls two beers from the bag and hands me one.

"Where did you get it?"

"My parents had a big party, and I lifted a six-pack. They weren't counting, so they'll never notice."

I try to imagine David sneaking around his house with a six-pack and hiding it in his room. Where would he hide it? Under his bed? In his sock drawer?

I try to twist off the top, but David is prepared. He pulls out a Swiss Army knife and pries off the caps.

"I don't think I want to drink more," I tell him. "The last time I got drunk was at my cousin's bar mitzvah. For some reason, the college student tending the bar was serving anyone over the age of thirteen. I guess he figured that we were adults by Jewish law so it was okay. I had five bourbon and gingers and threw up on the centerpiece."

"Your problem," David tells me as he readjusts his glasses, "is that you fear vomiting." He takes a big swig of his beer, and then continues in a very authoritative way for someone who, up until tonight, only drank soda. "Men vomit. Men are not afraid to toss the cookies, worship at the porcelain palace, chew the cud . . ." He waves his hand around, searching for more metaphors.

"Spit the multicolored rainbow?"

"Exactly." David opens his mouth as if he is about to

say something and lets loose a large belch. He smiles. "But if you don't wish to puke, it is important to burp," he tells me sincerely. "Keeps the gas from building up in your stomach."

I take a sip. "It's warm."

"It's not like I could keep it in the refrigerator. So when did you become a beer connoisseur? It's good. They drink it warm in England."

I don't think the English drink Bud Light warm, but I down some more to show I'm with him on this. David takes a few more glugs and makes a face. I don't think he's enjoying it much either.

"And we need to use more obscenities," David continues. He has obviously been thinking this through. "We don't cuss enough. How's the fucking beer?"

It's warm and tastes like thin mucus. "Fucking great," I say.

"Louder," commands David. "We should be loud. HOW'S THE FUCKING BEER?"

"FUCKING GREAT," I shout. It isn't much of a shout.

David drains about a third of his bottle. "And we should complain about our parents more."

"Yeah, parents suck."

We sit quietly. Since discussing Danielle's ass is off-limits, we are out of normal conversation.

David sighs and takes another pull from his bottle. I can tell he's trying to find words, but we don't know how to talk about much beyond school, parties, baseball.

"Feels like we've been a little off lately," he offers after a long silence.

"Sorry," I say. I'm not sure what I'm apologizing for.

I look at David. How is he still so David? How can this gay, non-cell-phone-carrying, pineapple-pizza-eating brown-bagger be so goddamned normal?

He nods and rubs his nose. "Me too," he says, but I'm not sure it's even an apology. Maybe this is the way real guys talk. It would be nice if we could manage longer sentences. Or more sentences.

I'm no better. I just shrug. We sit without talking. After a few minutes I'm desperate enough to bring up the prom.

"Carrie wants me to take Amanda to the prom."

"You told me. What's wrong with that?" David seems rejuvenated by the change in topic.

"Do I like Amanda?"

"You think she has nice tits."

Did I say that? I can't think of a good reason for me to have commented to David about Amanda's breast size, but I obviously had. "Does that make her a good prom date?"

"Does she want to go with you?"

"According to Carrie. She wants you to take M.C."

"Do you think she'd go with me?"

I'm not sure how to answer that question. I know that I'm only required to give a monosyllabic response indicating affirmation or denial, so it should be pretty easy, but it feels so complicated. I think the answer is yes, but the answer is only probably yes if M.C. thinks that David wants to date her, which he doesn't, so maybe I should say no, but that isn't quite right because I'm sure that if he asked her she would. I hear David sigh. A sigh is a verbal shrug.

"Look, it's no big deal," he says, as if he has been listening to my internal soliloquy. "I'd like to go to my prom and I get along really well with M.C. Why not?" All of which seems harmless enough.

"Are you going to tell her?" I ask.

I can't tell whether he's thinking or reacting. After a moment he gives a quiet "No."

Male mail

We drink two beers apiece, and then David drives me home. Two beers doesn't seem like too much, and we were sitting and talking for a while. I decide not to make a big deal of it now, but I was much happier riding with him when he only drank Diet Cokes.

"I sent you a letter," he tells me as we pull up in front of my house. "You'll probably get it soon."

"The kind with a stamp?"

David shrugs, then nods, then shrugs again. This is a

confusing mix of signals. He seems to have forgotten his non-verbal vocabulary.

"You see me every day, why did you send me a letter?"

"I had something to tell you."

"Oh," I say as if I understand. I don't think I want to ask.

"Just don't read it."

"You sent me a letter but you don't want me to read it?"

"Not yet. Wait. Okay?"

CHAPTER 16

Seven Rhetorical Questions
I Would Like Answered

If I know the answer, do I still have to ask?

For the record, Amanda does have nice tits, but when I see her at school on Tuesday I still feel like a jerk for having said so. She sits opposite me at lunch. We seem to be an item now, even though I still haven't officially asked her out, and she smiles at me several times but talks mostly to Carrie. M.C. has placed herself beside an empty chair, clearly intended for David, who doesn't look the least bit surprised when he arrives. The first thing he does when he sits down, even before he pulls out his ham sandwich, is turn to M.C. and say, "I was told I was supposed to ask you to the prom." She giggles and nods, and he says something like, "Well?" and she says, "I'd love to," and that seems to be that. They then spend the rest of lunch chatting. I mean, they've known each other for the better part of a year, and he gives her rides home all the time, but I didn't expect chatting. He appears to be enjoying the attention. Part of me wants to announce to the table that David isn't really interested in M.C.—mostly, I think, because he seems so much better at this than I am.

I can't get a word out. I've talked to Amanda before, but now that I know she's interested, I don't know what to say. I sit, barely speaking at all, and certainly not manipulating the conversation enough to give me an opening to ask her to the prom. Most of the discussion is focused on whether or not I will be suspended. This is not a topic I want to discuss. The general consensus is that I will have to write a letter of apology or something lame and nothing will happen to me. It is easy for everyone else to feel confident about that— seeing it isn't their butt that is hanging out in the wind.

Finally lunch is over and we go off to our classes. I feel like people are looking at me differently as we walk out of the cafeteria. Mitchell with a girlfriend is obviously a new Mitchell, one they don't recognize. Within twenty-four hours, everyone seems to know. Even Danielle, who's been sitting next to me in English all year without ever speaking to me, suddenly notices me, like maybe I've just material- ized in the seat beside her.

"How long have you been seeing Amanda?" she asks casually.

It takes me a moment to realize that she is addressing me and that I'm "seeing" Amanda.

"Not long," I say finally, turning some shade of bright red.

"She's cute," Danielle adds, managing to make the adjective sound like a put-down.

It is the longest conversation I have ever had with Danielle, and still I'm totally relieved when the substitute starts class.

Why only when someone is watching?

I'm supposed to be in calculus, but I have a migraine, which means I have to go to the office because my Fiorinal counts as a controlled substance and I'm not allowed to keep it in my locker. My migraines are a regular enough occurrence in calculus that Ms. Bexter waves me out without looking up from the homework she's grading. Ms. Bexter believes that people don't learn anything unless they learn it on their own, so her course mostly consists of handing out the textbooks, writing assignments on the board, and correcting papers. She always seems a little bitter about the fact that we don't understand what we are doing, but maybe that's just her personality. I get a lot of fifth-period migraines.

The J. P. Gilley water fountain is a lousy place to take my meds, but it works, which gives it a distinct advantage over the other two in the building. The Gilley fountain is centrally located, directly across from the girls' bathroom, so there's always a nice audience watching me choke and sputter as I try to swallow enough water to down the pills without spilling them out of my mouth.

Often they half melt and taste wretched, and I gag. Gagging is so cool.

Today I try to take both pills at once, a tricky maneuver but worth the risk if you can pull it off. I don't pull it off, and I have to spit the partially dissolved caplets back into my hand, where they sit in their little pool of drool happily disintegrating. As I'm about to try again, Danielle walks out of the girls' room. I consider dying as a reasonable alternative to standing there, palm extended, dripping medicated saliva. There is a pause, the world stops, and we look at each other longer than we would otherwise. I can tell she's been crying. She's fixed her makeup, but her eyes are still red. She stands in the doorway and stares at me as if she's never seen me before. I look back down at my Fiorinal, pop them in my mouth, and take a big swig of water. Thankfully, I keep them down this time. When I look up, she's still standing there.

"Migraine medication," I tell her.

"Bad?"

"I get them pretty often."

"Me too."

We have something in common. I almost forget to breathe.

She smiles at me, and I wonder if I'm still drooling. "I take Imitrex mostly," she says.

"Fiorinal."

"I tried that one." And with that, she smiles again and

walks away. I watch her walk down the hall, trying not to look like I'm just standing there watching her walk down the hall.

Of course, I get caught.

"Best ass in the school," Louis whispers conspiratorially. I hadn't even realized he was near me. "She knows we're watching. Walks like that aren't accidental."

I don't say anything. Okay, so I was watching her walk, and okay, I was looking at her butt, and okay, this is the second conversation I've had with Louis about this particular topic, and okay, I wasn't thinking about her personality or intellect, but God, am I as much of a sleaze as Louis?

"You can tell, you know, by the way she walks."

Tell what? Can I go to class now?

Louis doesn't wait for me to voice my questions. "Unlike your butt, that's no virgin ass."

I mutter something about how nice an ass it is.

Louis turns to me. "Mitch, you old party guy. You have it right. Life is a lot like Danielle's ass. You need to reach out and grab it. Know what I mean?"

Well, no.

Louis turns to me and pats my butt, gently, almost lovingly. "Just normal, everyday lust. Someday you too will know the pleasures of the flesh, my little friend. Till then, just keep yanking at it. Helps it grow."

He follows Danielle down the hall, swinging his hips in an exaggerated version of her walk.

Did Louis really just touch my butt?

Why are you such a prick?

David is in a bad mood. His baseball practice was canceled due to a threatened thunderstorm that has yet to appear, and driving me home isn't adequate compensation. It does not seem like a good time to ask him about the letter he mentioned earlier, despite the fact that it has me panicked. He already told me he was gay. *That* he could tell me at lunch. But this secret is so important that we have to go drink beer in a cul-de-sac so he can tell me about the existence of a letter that he doesn't even want me to read. A piece of paper in an envelope is making its way from a mailbox to a post office to my home, where it is supposed to wait, unopened, for something to happen. So, should we talk some more about the goddamned weather?

Instead I try to tell him about my magical encounter with Danielle. It doesn't come out right. I'm disappointed and say something like, "How come we never have real conversations?" and he tells me that a story about Danielle at the water fountain is not a real conversation and I accuse him of never being interested in what I'm feeling and he tells me I'm shallow and self-absorbed.

"Are you just in a bad mood?"

"Quite possibly," David answers, his eyes focused on the road. "Or maybe I'm just a prick."

"Prick" is another one of those words I'm not sure how to use. If I were normal, I'd call people pricks.

"Speaking of . . ." I pause, trying to summon the

129

word, but I can't even say it in front of David. "Thinking about people who are . . ."

"Pricks?"

"Yeah. Louis touched my butt. Is that weird?"

"Depends on the circumstances."

"We were discussing Danielle's butt at the time."

David doesn't feel the need to comment and focuses on driving us home.

"Why is Louis allowed to touch my butt and nobody thinks he's queer?"

"He's not queer. Queer is a gender expression. Boys that act or dress like girls and vice versa." David has obviously been doing some research. He goes on to answer the question I haven't asked. "I am gay, but my gender expression is male."

"What's my gender expression?"

"Nerd."

I wish he'd smile when he says things like that.

Can I refuse?

The phone rings. Carrie answers it and when I hear my name screeched I'm sure that it's Amanda, and I have a moment of total panic. I consider yelling back up the stairs that I'm in the bathroom but that would be even more embarrassing than having to talk to her. I pick up the phone and, despite my best effort to sound collected, my voice squeaks out a pathetic "hello." Not a "hi," not a "hey," not a "Mitchell here," but "hello."

"Hi, Mitchell." It's not Amanda. It takes a few brain cycles for the voice to register.

"M.C.?"

"Yeah, can we talk?"

I'm not sure I've ever heard M.C.'s voice over the phone.

"Sure," I say. Can I refuse?

"Has David talked about me at all?"

Okay, so M.C. is calling me to ask me about David. The answer is, of course, no, but even I know that I can't tell her that. "Sure, a little. I mean, not all the time, but some, of course. You know, guy talk." Guy talk?

"Do you think he likes me, or did he ask me out because Carrie pressured him into it?"

"Oh, he likes you." He said he liked her. Easy answer.

"Does he really like me, or is it just sort of a friend thing?"

Damn. I try to imagine what M.C. is doing on the other end of the line. She bites her lower lip when she gets nervous. I can almost picture the worried expression, but I can't fill in the rest of the picture.

"I mean, David is great, he really is, and I like him and all, but I didn't want him to think that I *really* liked him or was chasing him or something, because I wasn't. I mean, we don't even know each other that well, I mean we know each other, but we haven't really *gotten* to know each other, and I didn't want him to think I was just using him to go to the prom, because I'm not, but I didn't want him to get his expectations up, you know?"

Okay, she lost me there. Is she worried that David expects some sexual compensation in exchange for prom tickets? "I think David asked you because he likes to hang out with you. He said that you are fun to be around." He almost said that.

"So, mostly friends?" It is hard to tell if she is disappointed or relieved to hear that.

"I think so."

"Are you sure?"

I nod. Not that she can hear that on the phone.

"I just want him to like me. Not like *like* me, but like a friend. Boy, comma, friend, not boyfriend."

"You know, I think David already sees you as a . . . comma friend."

"Really?"

"Really."

"Really as in 'really' or really as in 'maybe I'll ask him,' or really because I'm a nutcase who you can't get off the phone?"

"Really, as in 'really.'"

There is another pause, but I don't volunteer anything more.

"So, what about Amanda?"

"Oh, I don't think David's interested in Amanda."

"No, you, stupid." She laughs. At least she recognized it as a joke.

I am so not into this. "I think she's . . . nice."

"Nice?"

"Great, cute, whatever?" At least I didn't mention her breast size.

"Are you interested in her?"

"Yeah."

"Are you going to ask her to the prom?"

"Do I have a choice?"

"Mitchell, of course you do. But you better do it soon. Look, I gotta go. See you tomorrow. Call her."

Who still uses note cards?

Carrie's also on my case about Amanda. She thinks I need to ask her out on a real date. I get out my note cards.

In eighth grade we had to take a health class. The boys were separated from the girls because who knows what mayhem might occur if we talked about sex in the same room. I don't know what the girls heard, but our class consisted mostly of lectures about how dangerous everything we might ever want to do would be. Smoke and you die of cancer. Drink and you die of liver disease, assuming you don't die in a car crash or shoot yourself from the inevitable depression that alcohol causes. French fries give you heart attacks. Sex causes STDs or, even worse, pregnancy, which would effectively end any chance you have of being successful at anything. Homosexuality was particularly evil since it immediately gave you AIDS, made you suicidal, and contributed to the destruction of traditional values, which led to godless Fascism or something. After the teachers had done their best to scare us into locking ourselves in our rooms until our post-college arranged marriages, we spent several weeks learning healthy, state-approved relationship tips. We had to role-play asking girls out on fun, wholesome dates, which was often pretty funny in an all-male class that was designed to promote healthy, chaste, heterosexual relationships. One of the suggestions, for those of us who were shy, was to write out note cards before you called. Everyone laughed at this idea. But now, given how tongue-tied I was when I ate lunch with Amanda, it seems to be worth a try.

On card one I write, "Hello, may I please speak to Amanda?" It sounds formal, but it seems safer than "Is Amanda home?" because who knows, I might get her parents or I might get Amanda and not recognize her voice, particularly if I'm nervous, or she might have a sister who sounds like her, and sometimes people just say "Hi" quickly and you can't be sure who it is that answered.

On card two I write, "How's it going?" It doesn't look right, so I rip it up, but I can't think of anything better, so I write it again on a new card. It still looks wrong. I decide to leave it for now.

On card three I write, "Not much," because I assume she'll ask me what's up with me. On the same card I write, "I was just wondering whether you'd like to go see *Rear Window* with me." Our one sort of artsy theater is doing a Hitchcock retrospective, and Amanda had said she liked Hitchcock. It seems pretty safe. I cross out "just" because it sounds like that's the only reason I'm calling, then write it back in because it sounds more conversational. I decide I'm perseverating. The reality is that I won't get the words out right anyway.

I put away the note cards. I am not calling Amanda.

What is wrong with me?

"I can't believe that you aren't asking Amanda to the prom." Carrie is pissed.

"I don't want to. I never told you I would."

"You didn't say you weren't going to. I already told her you would. What is wrong with you?"

Lots, actually. I look at my little sister, who is a good three inches taller than I am, and try to come up with a reasonable response. Then I try not to cry.

"You can't just push me around all the time. I can choose who I want to date."

"And what were you going to do, take David to the prom?"

As she glares at me, I say the only thing that comes to mind.

"He already has a date."

"Is the atomic weight of cobalt 58.9?"

"What happened with Amanda?" David asks me. We are lining up our storyboards in the chalk tray of the

135

blackboard that runs the length of the troll cave. It is about the only thing the board gets used for. We feel safe talking back here because all of the high-end computers are on the other side of the lab. We'd have to be shouting for someone to hear us.

"I didn't call her. Carrie already yelled at me about it."

"Why didn't you call her?"

"I didn't want to take her."

"So you're not going?"

"No."

"So you set me up to take M.C. so we can double-date for the prom, and now you aren't going?"

"Sort of."

"Sort of, my ass. Thanks, Mitchell. M.C. has never even sat in the front seat of my car, and I'm going to spend a buttload of money to take her to a dance I don't even want to go to . . ."

"Why'd you ask her?"

"Because I thought you wanted me to."

I could point out that I never told him to, that all I did was relay Carrie's plan, but he's already decided that it is all my fault.

"I'll take her."

"I already asked her. You can't just trade dates."

I hate it when David has a point. Besides, he said that he liked her and wanted to take her to the prom. I watch David set up a few more storyboards.

"You know, I don't know why you think you're gay."

"It's pretty simple, Mitchell. I'm gay because I like guys."

"Then why aren't you taking some guy to the prom?"

"Because I'm not dating any guys."

"Why not?"

"Same reason you aren't."

"I'm not because I'm not gay."

"Not the same reason you aren't dating guys, dumbass, the same reason you aren't dating *anyone*."

I think about that one for a second. "Because you're a pathetic loser with a nearly diagnosable personality disorder who is completely unappealing to the opposite, or in your case, the same sex?" I suggest.

"No, I take it back. For a different reason."

"Explain."

"Do I have to?"

"Yes."

"It's mathematics."

"Now I'm really not believing you."

"Hold on. It's not calculus; it's more like set theory. Remember Venn diagrams—the little overlapping circles? Circle 1 is straight males, circle 2 is males I know who are gay and willing to admit they are, and circle 3 is males I like." David draws the three overlapping circles on the chalkboard. He does not label them.

"At this moment the one little area of overlap that counts, this intersection here," he says, pointing, "males who will admit that they are gay, and whom I also like, that little piece of the diagram is empty. Not a name. Therefore, no dates."

I stare at the chalkboard and think about what David is saying. It seems like a very specific, very small niche.

CHAPTER 17

Letters

USPS

There are two envelopes waiting for me when I get home. I pick them both up and take them to my room. I place them on my desk. I stare at them. I start to get up so I can go do something else, homework or watching television. I sit back down. I open the first one. I look at it, refold it, and place it back in its envelope. I leave the second one unopened on my desk and rummage around in my backpack for my calculus book. I sit back down at my desk. I open the second envelope.

SAT

Knock on the door. I start to get up, but before I get out of my chair the door opens and my sister is standing by my desk.

"So, what did you get? I saw the envelope when I got home, so don't pretend it didn't come."

"I don't have to tell you, Carrie."

"Sure you do. Everyone tells their scores." Carrie's height advantage is intimidating enough when we are standing; with me sitting, she totally towers over me. I fight the urge to adjust my desk chair to a taller position.

"I really don't want to talk about this right now."

"That bad."

"Not that bad."

"So sort of middle of the road. Not Princeton, but not community college material." Carrie picks up my battery-powered pencil sharpener and turns it over, watching the shavings collect in the plastic top. A CPA snow globe. She's waiting for my answer.

"I'm not telling you."

"So it can't be good." Tired of standing, Carrie finds butt room on the corner of my desk. She turns the sharpener back over and begins to sharpen my already sharp pencils.

"It could be good, but I'm not telling you."

"How good can it be if you aren't telling me?" She looks up from the pencil sharpener and raises both eyebrows.

"It could be very good even if I'm not telling you." So there.

"But it isn't very good, is it? It's only somewhat good? Am I right?"

She's right. The score is perfectly respectable, but not amazing.

"Why didn't you check it online? You did, didn't you? But you didn't tell Mom and Dad! Ooh—you have changed. When did you get so sneaky? Sneaky—or just embarrassed?"

Embarrassed. I know what Mom and Dad would say. They would be proud of me. They would tell me they were proud of me even if I had bombed the thing. I look down at the desk to avoid confirming her suspicions. David's letter.

"I don't think I want to continue this conversation," I tell her as nonchalantly as I can. I look her directly in the eyes and try to slip David's letter underneath my calculus book.

"Who wrote you a letter?" Carrie makes a grab at it, but I pull it away.

"Would you go away!"

Carrie makes her pucker face, a mix of bewildered and pissed-off. "Love letter? No, no female would write you a love letter in pencil."

"Go away."

"Suddenly full of secrets. I'm your sister, you can tell me."

"Please go away."

My voice sounds more desperate than angry. I think Carrie realizes that she has somehow pushed this too far and she backs off, but not apologetically.

"Geez, I was only asking."

www.atomfilms.com

David and I sit on the couch in the living room watching a DVD of *Pib and Pog* episodes that Wallman lent us about three months ago. Eventually, we'll have to give it back. We are drinking Diet Coke and eating cold pizza left over from the aftermath of one of my mother's cooking disasters. We aren't talking much, but we never talk during the show. We might miss something we didn't catch before in the twenty times we've already watched Pib slice off Pog's face with a large chef's knife.

He must know I got the letter, but I haven't told him I got it. He must have guessed that I read it. We both pretend that nothing is different.

Is something different?

S

There are two Davids: the one who will letter in baseball and the one who hangs out with me. Sometimes I get them confused.

Baseball David has lots of friends. Not that he spends time with any of them, but when they pass each other in the hall they do this weird touch-knuckles-and-bump-into-each-other routine that I assume is sports-related. Baseball David is the one who takes me along to parties and finds me a beer to drink so I don't look like a total loser.

The other David is the one who reassures me about my pending expulsion by listing famous people who never finished high school. This David is sort of an anti-Superman. Superman dives into phone booths, rips off the drab suit, and emerges with the *S* emblazoned on his chest. Drab is not David's disguise.

Which one wrote me the letter? Is there a third David?

◉ ◉ ◉

David calls me later to ask about some assignment, but it feels like more of an excuse than a question. We talk about some asinine thing Thad said in the hallway. The conversation is over but neither of us have said good-bye. I know I'm supposed to say something about the letter, but since I wasn't supposed to have read it, I'm not sure what to say. Telephone silence. I have let it go on too long to pretend it doesn't mean something.

Q and A
"Did you get the letter?"
  "Yes."
  "Did you read it?"
  "Yes."
  "Do you want to talk about it?"
  "No."

ASAP
Life would be a lot easier if we could schedule our crises. I can give you from 3:30 to 5:45 tomorrow to discuss our

lives, but then I need to pick my sister up from a friend's house, have dinner, and study for my calculus test. If I finish early, we could talk on the phone between 10:48 and 11:10, but no later or I'll fall asleep during history— and Kalikowski has started to notice that I often fall asleep during her class. If you give me a ride to school tomorrow, we can talk as we walk from the parking lot, but I can't afford to be late to first period again. If that isn't enough, I can try to schedule a good chunk of time for emotional outpourings early next week after my history paper is due and after I find out whether I've been expelled.

OK

More silence.

David breaks first. "I think I would like to talk about it."

"Okay."

"Should I come over there?"

"Okay."

"Would you rather meet somewhere else?"

"No, here is okay."

"Now?"

"Yeah, I guess. No. Can we wait?"

More silence. This one sounds impatient.

"I'd like some time," I say. "How about this weekend? Friday? We could go grab some pizza and talk."

There's a code here. Friday is two days away, which is

admittedly blowing him off, but we have set aside time, and it is a weekend evening. This means we are still friends. I said we will talk. It is a promise that I will deal with it.

"Sure, that makes sense. Yeah," David answers. Three affirmatives in a row but not one of them sounds convincing.

RE:

I look at the letter. I know it is in English, but I still don't know how to read it.

David says we already have a relationship, we just don't admit it. I looked up the word "relationship" in the dictionary. It can mean a lot of things.

David says he feels like we are more than friends. He does not attach a list describing the ways in which what we do goes beyond friendship. He does not say he considers me his boyfriend, just his best friend. He says he knows I'm not gay. Is he hoping that I'll change? If he did fall in love with someone else, would we still be friends? How would I be different from the guy he is in love with? It can't be all about sex.

There's a lot here about needing to describe what he's feeling. He uses the word "feeling" a lot. Nothing in this letter actually tells me *what* he's feeling, just that he needs to tell me. I think there are some words missing.

RSVP

The pizza place is a little too public, so we swing through the drive-through and pick up cheeseburgers and drive over to the cul-de-sac where we drank beers the other night. The weather, which had been so nice lately, has turned and it is too cold to eat outside, so we eat in David's car. I don't take off my seat belt and neither of us turns to face the other, so the entire conversation takes place as if we are performing for an audience watching through the windshield.

I start.

"I read your letter. This doesn't have to be a big deal. I know you're gay. I've known for a long time. I told you already that I'm fine with it."

"This isn't about me being gay."

"It's about me not being gay."

David takes a long breath like he's about to say something that he's hidden somewhere deep inside himself and he needs extra air to speak it now.

"Has it ever occurred to you that this may not be about you? I'm not gay to annoy you. I'm not gay because of you. At some point has it ever flickered across your consciousness that it might be more difficult to be a gay seventeen-year-old than to have a gay friend?"

"You always seem okay." I don't mean to sound defensive, but if he has been having such a hard time, he hasn't shown it much.

"I am okay. But you aren't helping much."

I stare out the windshield. "I thought, from your note, that this was about me."

"It was about us. Who we are."

"We're friends, aren't we?"

"Just friends?"

The phrase has the crisp snap of rejection. I swallow hard. Are we "just friends"? I want to tell him not to demean the word. Not make it sound so flimsy and insubstantial.

"Still friends?"

It starts to rain. Ugly, loud, angry drops of rain. It moves over the car in waves, drowning out anything we might have said. If we were talking. I have an irrelevant moment of revelation in which I realize that the phrase "heavy silence" is an excellent description of how much presence silence has when you sit with someone and don't talk. It is the most present absence I have ever felt.

"Yes," he says after way too long.

David starts the car and drives to my house. He pulls the car into the driveway, but neither of us speaks.

I want to do something. I want to change the topic. I want to talk about our calculus homework or whether Wallman ever bathes or whether he thinks I have a shot at getting into Princeton. I want to laugh. Why can't we laugh?

Or cry. I can't imagine David crying. I've never seen him cry—except that one time in fourth grade when we got into a fight and I punched him and he cried and I cried even though he hadn't punched me back. I still can't remember why I punched him. Is it a fight if only one of you is fighting? Fighting doesn't seem like something you can do by yourself. A little like love.

I want to scream. I want to be angry and scream. I want David to say something.

I close my eyes for a moment, listening to the rain, trying hard to find some counterpart in my experience for this moment, something that will let me know how I am supposed to respond. There must be a right answer, some magic words that will open up this car door and let me out and let me go on with my life. I know so many stories, so many scripts—but this moment isn't in any of them. I don't know what we are doing here. I don't know what I should say. I know we will eventually leave this car and on Monday we will go to school and eat lunch together, and David will give me half of his roast beef sandwich (the smaller half). I will go watch him sit on the bench at his next home game. He will give me rides home from school. We will go see movies. We will eat pizza.

When we start talking again, it is in quiet voices of resignation and lies. David says he wrote the letter because he felt he needed to tell me how he feels, but he didn't expect anything to change. I tell him that I now know how he feels, but it doesn't change anything. What we mean is that both of us will pretend that nothing is different, and wait for something to change.

CHAPTER 18

Two More Theories About Curtis and a Car Ride with Louis

Theory 2: I got Curtis fired (Mitchell version)

Finally, over a week after I turned in my offensive DVD, Sorrelson's administrative assistant comes to get me in the middle of calculus. Although I haven't said anything about my last meeting, everyone already seems to know I'm in trouble and why. Curtis has officially taken a leave of absence and we are on our fourth sub. This one is an older woman who seems very angry almost all the time. Her primary objection seems to be the school smoking policy, which forces her to walk off the campus grounds in order to smoke. Class starts punctually six minutes late and ends six minutes early, as it takes twelve minutes to walk to the edge of the campus, smoke her cigarette, and walk back. We mostly wait quietly in our seats, being the passive good doobie sheep we are. At least she has read the book.

Mr. Sorrelson's lower lip is sticking out again when I

arrive. At first he ignores me and continues reading some memo, the single sheet of paper on his vast desk. The memo looks to me like it's only about ten lines long, but he leaves me standing there for several minutes while he studies it. Either the whole thing is for dramatic effect or he should never have been allowed out of third grade.

"Please sit down, Mitchell," he commands with his gruff formality, as if he has just that moment realized I've been standing there.

I sit down. Pay no attention to the man behind the curtain. It occurs to me that Louis has misquoted the movie and that it doesn't fit this situation at all, but repeating it to myself over and over again is strangely comforting.

Sorrelson sighs deeply and begins again in his painfully slow gurgling voice. "I have watched your cartoon." He pauses for a reaction. I can't think of a good one, so I just sit there and wait. "And I am disappointed in you. This is not what we expected from a young man of your accomplishments. I am sure that you meant it as a harmless prank, a kind of joke, but you are old enough to take other people's feelings into account before you act. Now I feel as if, perhaps, we may have been mistaken about your character. We will now have to bear that in mind when we write your college recommendation letters."

Ouch.

"I also spoke to your parents." He pauses again for a

reaction. "I believe that I was able to make them see the gravity of this situation." He obviously hasn't spoken to my mother. I wait out his next pause.

"I feel that, given the seriousness of this offense, I have no choice but to refer the issue to our Judicial Board."

Cue the scary music. The Judicial Board is a group of five students and two faculty members who review breaches of the school's honor code. They don't get to wear black robes, and all they can really do is recommend disciplinary actions to the headmaster/CEO, who ignores them a good half of the time, but it is never a good thing to be sent to the J-Board. The student positions are all elected, and I think people do it mostly because it looks good for colleges. I can't even remember who we elected this year. I have an uneasy feeling that it might have been Louis.

Sorrelson is looking at his calendar. "The Judicial Board usually meets on Tuesdays during activity period, and obviously we've already missed today. Let's see, because of the holiday, next Tuesday is a Monday schedule, but we could try to get them together on Wednesday . . . but no, wait, Wednesday is a flex day because of an assembly, but we do have a Tuesday on Tuesday that next week, I think. Yes. Right. Two weeks from today. 11:20. They meet in my office."

How? Does everyone stand? Do people sit on the desk?

"I assume you are aware of how this works. The Judicial Board will ask you questions, then they meet and discuss what they have heard secretly, I mean without you, and then they will make a recommendation to Dr. VandeNeer. I'm sure he will want to meet with your parents to discuss any disciplinary actions we may need to take. You may return to class."

"Thank you," I say as I leave, since he seems to be waiting for me to say something. Why do I keep thanking this man?

I must look pretty shellshocked when I return to calculus, because even David notices. Luckily, lunch is next.

If anything has changed since our car ride over the weekend, it is hard to tell from the way David's acting. Over the last two days we have talked about homework, baseball, and Curtis's sub, and he has done his Pib and Pog voices about sixty times. Nothing unusual. David is sitting at lunch with his sandwich and apple, waiting for me with the same slightly bored look on his face that he always has when I take too long at my locker. He looks a little less disinterested when I fill him in on the details of my conversation with Sorrelson.

"I hate to agree with Louis, but he's right. What are they going to do to you?" David sounds convincing, like he really knows about these things. "The J-Board is a complete joke. And there is no way Sorrelson is going to poison your college recommendations. Your parents would sue."

I nod, but all I'm really thinking is, "Shit, I have ruined my entire future by showing a cartoon to my English class." You would think it would be harder to screw up this badly.

David is looking at me with an expression that conveys the depth of his sincerity and concern. I'm thinking of punching him, but he seems to remember who he is suddenly and makes a typical David comment: "Some school will take you. It's not like you're serving jail time or something. Plus, you know, there are lots of jobs that don't require a college degree."

Jobs. A wave of guilt-induced nausea brings the taste of vomit to my mouth. I manage to keep it down and breathe loudly through my nose.

"Are you okay?" David asks. "You look like you're about to color the carpet."

I nod, without opening my mouth. "It's not just me," I explain between long breaths. "They fired Curtis for letting me show the thing. I'm sure that's why he's gone. I got someone fired. I got Curtis fired."

I can't finish lunch. Instead I treat myself to a lie-down in the nurse's office. I'm the only one over twelve who still uses the cot. She takes my temperature and gives me Pepto-Bismol and a few clucking noises. I can't tell if the clucking indicates sympathy or disapproval, but she leaves me in the little room and turns off the light. I lie in the darkness, wondering what professional options pompous, recently fired English teachers and pathologically shy, recently expelled teenagers have.

Theory 3: I got Curtis fired (M.C. version)

The nurse's office is by the sophomore lockers. When I do finally get myself off the cot, I have to pass by M.C.'s locker, which at this moment has M.C. in front of it. She's not, however, simply standing in front of it; she seems to be engaged in some form of tug-of-war with it. It is hard to tell whether she is trying to put her backpack in or take it out, because she's smashing it viciously with the door. When the bag has been punished enough, she yanks it loose, which precipitates a rainstorm of books, notebooks, loose paper, and various articles of clothing. She picks up some of what has escaped, opens the latch, and tries to toss it in before more falls out. So far, this does not appear to be a successful strategy. I help by picking up a shoe and a French book and tossing them into the locker, but the shoe misses the mark and bounces back into the hallway. It isn't until I retrieve the shoe that I notice she's crying.

"Maybe you should just take a few minutes and clean out your locker. It can't take that long."

"Stupid fricking locker," she snorts, and slams it again. The door catches on her binder and the locker vomits most of its contents onto the floor. M.C. sinks to the floor next to the pile of debris and lets loose a wail.

"I'll help," I say, and I start picking up the larger books. M.C. reaches up, grabs my hand, and tugs me down beside her.

"Forget the locker. Who cares about the locker?" She looks at me, tears streaming down her freckles. "I am a horrible person."

"You are?" This is a dumb response, and I know it is a dumb response even before it comes out of my mouth.

"I got Curtis fired," she tells me, and looks away again.

"No, you didn't." I feel pretty sure of this since I'm convinced that *I'm* the one who got Curtis fired.

"He didn't do anything, I mean we didn't do anything. Nothing. Nothing at all. I mean, I wanted to do something, not everything but something, but I didn't even try to do anything."

I am still stuck on the idea that M.C. wanted to do anything with Curtis and I am now totally flustered. She looks up for some sort of response and the only thing she can read on my face is horror. She begins to sob.

And I'm stuck. I know that this hallway will soon be full of people. I'm not sure what they will make of the two of us sitting on the floor beside the spilled contents of M.C.'s locker. And what am I supposed to do about M.C.? I think I should hold her hand or give her a hug or something, but I'm not sure how to do that. Her hands are currently wrapped around her waist like she is giving herself a hug. I pat her on the back, a little too forcefully, like maybe I'm trying to burp her or something, but she responds by leaning into me a little. My arm is sort of draped over her shoulder, but my hand hangs limply in the air, too far to rest on her shoulder but not far enough to reach her arm. I flail a little, then leave it hanging there.

Now that the physics are out of the way, I try working up a verbal response.

"M.C., what are we talking about?"

"Carrie said that David said that you said that Curtis was fired. I thought he just had some sort of nervous breakdown or was outed or something."

"He wasn't fired because of you. I don't even know that he was fired."

"Well, what if someone thought something had happened because maybe someone else had hinted that something *could* happen, even if it didn't, and then didn't deny it when other people thought maybe it had? I am such a jerk. I should have just said it—I should have just said that nothing happened. We painted flats together in the workroom and we barely spoke, but it felt personal, romantic and all and I'm sure I looked flushed and then Charlotte made a joke about me being all flushed but it was all like joking, nobody actually asked if we had done anything, and now, and now . . . crap."

"I don't think that they could fire him just because of a rumor. You would have had to complain or something."

"Then what happened? Why did he just leave in the middle of class?"

"I don't think he left because you painted flats together and Charlotte made a joke. It doesn't make sense."

Then I tell her how *I* got Curtis fired, and while she doesn't quite buy it, at least it's enough to make her doubt her own theory a little and get us off the floor. We shovel most of her belongings back into her locker and, through some miracle of gravity, most of it stays in long enough for her to shut the door.

She wipes her eyes, looks me full in the face.

"Nothing happened. You believe me, don't you?"

I tell her I do.

"I really didn't want anything to happen. I just thought he was cute."

I tell her I believe her.

"I really have to grow up."

It is almost painful to see M.C. being this serious.

"I'll see you at home," she says, and starts off down the hall.

Has she moved in?

Have you noticed that Louis always has an answer?

The school has become an obstacle course. Once past the M.C. locker of despair, I find myself blocked by the large Louis of obstinance. He has witnessed something, but he's not sure what. M.C. crying. Me with my arm around her.

"Stud boy, getting a little frisky there?"

"She was upset."

"I would have cried too if you put your arm around me. I know, I know, you're late for class. Do me a favor,

158

though. Let me give you a ride home. I have a question for you."

I almost suggest that he could write me a letter, but it's a joke he wouldn't get. I don't have a ride home, so I accept. Has to be better than talking to him now.

Louis drives a car so old, so decrepit, so noisy, that it's almost cool. I can see road beneath my feet through the rusted floorboard. The car smells of beer and farts, and the backseat is a trash dump. I hold my backpack on my lap.

When he asks why M.C. was upset, I explain in abbreviated form that she thought she might be responsible for Curtis being fired.

"Curtis wasn't fired," Louis says simply.

"How do you know?"

"Wrong euphemism. You've got to learn admin speak. The notice said he was on personal leave. Personal means he either went wacko and needed time off or someone kicked it and he's grieving somewhere. I'm betting wacko. If he was fired, they would have said he was on administrative leave."

Strangely, I feel better. Maybe I'm a little sorry someone died or my teacher had a nervous breakdown, but at least neither of those options are my fault.

"You know M.C. pretty well, right?" Louis asks, not looking at me but not exactly paying a lot of attention to the road either.

"I guess."

"Ever . . . you know?"

"No."

"Nothing, never?"

"No."

"Why not? She's not a bra-buster or anything, but she's cute. Definitely cute. Butt like that you could squeeze yourself into. Am I right?"

"Sure, I mean, yeah. But it would be weird. She's been Carrie's best friend since they were about five."

"Like kissing your sister."

No. Not at all. But M.C. is, well, M.C. I've known her forever; she practically lives in my house. To her I'm somewhere between furniture and a relative. I don't feel like explaining any of this to Louis, who doesn't look like he's paying attention anyway. "No. She's just a friend."

"So you aren't taking her to the prom?"

So *this* is where this conversation is going. I am so relieved to tell him that David has already asked her.

"Can't quite see her with your sidekick," Louis says, sounding slightly disappointed. "Smells like he was pistol-whipped into it. Shotgun wedding?"

"Carrie."

"That makes sense. Who was your assignment?"

"Amanda. But I didn't ask her."

"Now *she* is busting her seams. Short, but compact. Everything handy, but probably more than you can handle. Scared you shitless, right?"

"Are you planning on going to the prom?"

"Thanks for the invite, but I have someone I'm supposed to take, church youth group girl, although I would have dumped her for M.C. We've gone out a couple of times and she knows the prom is coming and if I don't take her it would be a big deal."

Church youth group? Louis is part of a church youth group? Someone who goes to a church is willing to go out with Louis? I look back over at him as he steers his car down my street. He has some purposeful fuzz growing on his chin that may be an attempt at cultivating facial hair, but he still looks like Louis. Doesn't sound like him, though. Maybe we've never had a real conversation.

"I feel sort of stuck. She's really fun. She's funny. We haven't gotten very far, but I never really do. I'm not a guy who they're lining up to fuck, if you know what I mean. I can get them to laugh, but no one ever laughs their pants off. Ugly, fat, deformed—you name it, I've dated it, and I can't even get burn victims to lick me."

I'm not feeling particularly sorry for Louis.

"You can't get it either, can you?"

There doesn't seem to be any reason to lie.

"No," I say quietly.

"Not even kissing. I mean, other than your sister."

"Not even with."

"Sad. On the other hand, virginity isn't so bad. Keeps your wrist muscles supple. But you're not a bad-looking guy, Mitchell. A little scrawny, but very sincere. At some point, you've got to take a chance." Louis pulls his car into my driveway. "Just by the by, could you not mention to M.C. that I asked about her? It would make it awkward, you know."

I promise him I won't, although I can't imagine Louis feeling awkward around anyone. I thank him for the ride and he takes off, a smelly stream of gray smoke pouring out of his tailpipe.

CHAPTER 19

Mitchell Gets a Haircut

The theological implications of barbering,
part one: free will

M.C. seems to be staring at me. She, Carrie, and I are all doing our homework in the family room, although Carrie decided that she could work better on the couch, watching television. She is holding her French book; maybe that counts as studying. It is Friday afternoon, so there's not a lot of pressure to get things done. I don't know who we think we're fooling. M.C. and I are sitting on opposite ends of the table and I really want to know if I'm just imagining that she's staring at me, but I can't figure out how to look up without meeting her eyes, so I stay focused on the page in front of me, which hasn't become any clearer in the five minutes I have been staring at it. I try a half glance, but I can't get my eyes up far enough to see beyond her chest, which makes me feel even more awkward. M.C. is pretty thin, but she does have a noticeable shape underneath her T-shirt, even if she isn't what Louis would call a "bra-buster." This isn't the first time I've noticed.

I look up at Carrie on the couch, as if I've just thought of something I need to say to her, but she isn't looking in my direction, so I give a little shake of my head as if I thought of something and then decided not to say it. I contemplate making a little chuckle but decide against it. My head now up, I turn casually toward M.C., who *is* staring at me. This seems easier for her.

"You need a haircut, Mitchell," she decrees. "Do you want me to do it for you? I'm not sure I can stand that cowlick sticking up in the back much longer."

"Thanks for the input, but I think I'll go to the barbershop. No offense."

"Not that creepy place you and your dad always go. Have you ever noticed that you are the only ones over seven or under sixty that go there? They always cut your hair too short. You look like a refugee from the late fifties. You need a *real* haircut."

My hair is a frequent target of derision and instruction, but most of the previous advice I've gotten has centered around mousse, gel, and blow-drying. Once Carrie tried to get me to dye it, but we've never focused on my choice of stylists before. Carrie and M.C. change their hair color almost as often as their clothes. Nothing too strange, mostly natural shades, highlights, darkening, streaks. I will not let either of them touch my hair.

And to be fair, I no longer go to Tony's, my dad's barbershop. About two years ago I abandoned that bastion of archaic *Reader's Digests* for one of the Excellent Cuts chain. Graduating to Excellent Cuts was a proud moment of independence. I'm treated as an adult there. They call me "sir," as in, "You are next, sir." I don't have to discuss baseball or be told how much I've grown every time I go in. Plus, the haircuts are pretty cheap.

"I like my haircuts," I tell M.C., doing my best to summon some conviction.

"You can't go to the prom with geek hair."

"I'm not going to the prom. And it's not geek hair."

"It's the same haircut you've had since you were six, Mitchell," Carrie interjects from the couch, without looking up. "Geek hair."

M.C. gets up and returns to the table with the phone book and the phone.

"We can't take him anywhere too radical, we won't get him through the door." She is addressing Carrie. I have been third-personed again. "What about that place down near Walgreens—sort of near the Chinese restaurant. What's it called?" She begins thumbing through the Yellow Pages.

I look down at my calculus homework as if it might hold the answer, or an answer, any answer. I am not letting Carrie and M.C. take me to some salon to get my hair cut. I try several times to voice this decision, but I can't get their attention.

"They have an opening now, but we have to hurry," M.C. tells me as she hangs up the phone and slips on her sweater. "What? Oh, don't even pretend you aren't coming. It'll be great."

Why are you doing this? Why are you doing this to me? Why am I letting you do this to me?

"You can't be scared about getting your hair cut. What are you, four? Carrie and I could drag you bodily into the car and strap you into the chair, but that might be more embarrassing. Or, I'm sure there are some scissors around here somewhere."

Lamb to the slaughter, I stand up and follow M.C. to the car.

The theological implications of barbering, part two: predestination

Soiree is not Tony's. It isn't Excellent Cuts. From the moment we walk through the door, I know that this is a mistake.

First of all, I think I am the only male in the salon. Tony's was all-male. There were always three or four old men who came to have their few remaining hairs shortened and a few young boys waiting to lose their curls, accompanied by their mothers. The mothers are only tolerated at Tony's as transportation. At Excellent Cuts, there are always both men and women. The waiting area is basic airport lounge decor, all very comfortable. Soiree looks more like a cave. It is dark and full of chrome, and loud techno music, audible from the parking lot, emanates from its walls. It's also crowded. Women wearing black bathrobes wait on benches and talk at the juice bar or sit in the chairs with what looks like tin foil in their hair.

At Soiree, everyone has a name. M.C. tells the receptionist, who introduces herself as Julie and whose fingernails are at least as long as her fingers, that we have an appointment with Alex. She tells us that Alex will be with us in a moment. This appears to be Julie's sole function. With those nails, I'm pretty sure she can't hold a pencil or type, so telling people to wait must be her only job. She seems good at it.

As we wait, Carrie explains that lots of salons have coffee and juice bars and yes, that is tin foil but no, I won't need to have a tin foil treatment. I do need to change into one of the black bathrobes and have my hair washed by Anna, who seems to be a hair washer. I try to explain that I've already washed my hair today, but that seems irrelevant. After about fifteen years of practice, I'm pretty good at washing my own hair, but even I have to admit that Anna does a really nice job. It helps that she isn't much older than me and that she smiles when I don't know where to sit or what to do. In the end, I don't need to do much, just lie back and let her massage my scalp with the shampoo and rinse it off. She wraps a towel around my head and sends me back to Carrie and M.C.

I'm a little freaked out about having to wait for Alex. At Excellent Cuts, everyone has name tags, but you don't request anyone. It's an assembly line; you just wait for the next opening. Here no one wears name tags, and you wait to be introduced. I can see what happens next. Once you are introduced, then you have a relationship. If I come back, and don't make an appointment with Alex, he or she might be hurt. I will always have to ask for Alex now. If I don't come back, Alex will wonder what happened to me. His or her feelings might be hurt. I am going to have to come back and have my hair cut by Alex now for the rest of my life. I do not want to have my hair cut by someone with a name.

We sit. We wait. My 4:30 appointment, which we were told to hurry for, doesn't commence until almost six, but no one seems fazed by the delay. Eventually Julie smiles at us and tells us that Alex is ready, and we are escorted to a chair and introduced to this person named Alex who will cut my hair. I'm pretty sure Alex is female, but I'm not completely convinced. Alex is bald, dressed in jeans and a bright-colored T-shirt, and has several prominent piercings: nose, lips, cheek, and eyebrow. None of this strikes me as a good sign. What does it say about her attitude toward hair that she has chosen not to have any? It occurs to me that my father's barber is also named Alex, although he looks more like an Earl.

I sit quietly while Carrie and M.C. explain to Alex that I need to have my hair cut in a standard nerdy fashion, because otherwise I'll freak (like I'm not freaking already), but if she could make it more cool nerdy rather than geek nerdy, it might get me going in the right direction.

Alex nods as if she understands. She then takes out a giant clipper and shaves off a huge swath of my hair.

I don't remember my first haircut, but I know I cried a lot. We have a picture. I don't look happy in it. It is all I can do not to repeat that performance now. I look at M.C., who is smiling, almost proudly, like I'm some kind of science project that she expects to win first prize with at the next fair.

Carrie is thumbing through fashion magazines and talking about layering. Alex is busily removing more hair. It falls in giant clumps on the cloth in front of me. I don't look up to see myself in the mirror; I'm not ready to know what I look like bald.

We have waited for close to two hours, but the actual haircut takes less than ten minutes. Alex rubs some sort of gel in my now very short hair. Or at least parts of it are short. Some of the hair on top has been left longer. I'm assuming it's intentional, but it looks like Alex forgot to cut random tufts of hair, which now stick up at odd angles on top of my head. Alex, M.C., and Carrie seem quite pleased. I am horrified.

"How do you like it? Isn't it great?" gushes M.C.

"Much better. Who knew you could look good?" Carrie adds.

"You should come back in about three weeks," Alex tells me. "Otherwise it will grow out funny. I'll have Julie schedule you an appointment."

Julie also seems to take the money. I almost choke when she charges me forty-five dollars. Carrie reminds me that I need to go tip both Alex and Anna, and reassures me that it would be more expensive if I were a girl.

"They always let guys off easy at these places," she explains as we leave.

On the way out I steal another glance at one of the mirrors lining the walls, hoping maybe I had missed something the first time.

"It looks really good," M.C. tells me, and it sounds like a genuine compliment.

The theological implications of barbering, part three: purgatory and egg rolls

Still, they must feel a little guilty, because we stop for Chinese takeout on the way home and Carrie uses her cell phone to call David. She doesn't ask me first, which is probably good since I would have told her not to. But it's probably better if David comes over, because that's what he would have done if this haircut had been inflicted upon me last week instead of this week. David is trying hard to be pre-letter normal, so when we get home, I try to look happy to see him. He is waiting on the porch. David always waits outside.

"What the hell happened to you?" he asks as I get out of the car. I stop pretending to be happy to see him.

"He looks great," Carrie tells David, as if this were a fact and he was just a little slow to figure it out.

"Did you pay money for that?" Dad asks, meeting us at the door. He looks rumpled, as if he just woke up.

"He looks great," Carrie explains again, with an audible sigh. Everyone is so dense.

"Chinese food?" Dad asks, sniffing the air and then noticing the telltale white boxes we're carrying. "Mom should be home soon. Let's set the table."

As I walk by, Dad tries to give my hair a friendly ruffle, but the gel has made it stiff and a little sticky, so it doesn't really move. "Looks great, Mitchell," he tells me, without much conviction. "A whole new you."

⊙　⊙　⊙

David and I choose to eat our dinner on the front stoop, and since I am in haircut recovery, no one objects. David is telling me something about global warming. I'm not listening. I keep touching the back of my head, feeling for the missing hair. He seems impatient with me.

"Your hair's fine. Stop playing with it."

"It's not fine. It's not me, and I'm not happy with it."

He shrugs. "It grows back. It's not like you lost a limb."

"Thanks a lot."

"What's your problem?"

"I am not having a good day, okay? And you aren't helping much."

"What do you want me to do? I can't glue your hair back on."

"You don't have to fix it. I just want to be allowed to be pissed off. I'm depressed. I'm actually depressed by this haircut. Seriously, authentically, honestly, and completely desolated."

"We could always shave your head."

I throw an egg roll at David in actual anger. He looks at me and laughs. It's the first laugh I've heard out of him in a long time. I find myself smiling too. There is something inherently funny about throwing egg rolls.

CHAPTER 20

Almost Poetry—A Party in Five Haiku

David feels guilty.
Pickup at 8:00 sharp.
We party tonight.

I must have made David feel guilty, or maybe he's just trying hard to show that nothing is different between us, because he e-mails me on Saturday afternoon. E-mail turns out to be the best way to contact me, because Carrie is permanently attached to our phone. David's e-mails read exactly the way David talks. Monotone, slightly annoyed, suitable for telegrams, as if he paid by the word.

Recovered from haircut? Josh house party tonight. Pickup @ 8:00?

Not gushing, but I can hear the overtones of a guilty conscience in it. He even rounded off the pickup time. A non-apologetic David would have offered to get me at 8:04. I reply in the same style.

Hair OK. Party OK. 8:00 OK.

Almost poetry.

A stifling, noisy
box of poorly packed people;
there is no order.

Josh's house is a stifling, noisy box of poorly packed people. There is no order to the arrangement of bodies and no flow to their movements. David and I stand in our usual spot, but tonight we have company because most of the baseball team is here. David is conversant in at least three different sports, one for each season, but baseball is the only one he really knows. I nod a lot and sip the same can of lukewarm beer I have held all evening. Without explanation, David is back to drinking Diet Coke and is on his third. I decide not to mention it. I look around for Mariel, because I am so sick of talking about baseball, but she doesn't seem to be here. I ask David about it during a sports pause and he shrugs.

"She has a boyfriend. Chapel Hill. She's been down there a lot."

"Since when?"

"A couple of weeks." He shrugs again. Not sure what the second shrug is supposed to mean. It's not surprising that Mariel has a boyfriend, or that she's dating someone in college. I guess it also makes sense that she would have told David and not me. I do wonder whether it felt awkward for either of them. Now there's a guy that's not David in her life. Are the two guys in separate categories, or are they on a continuum and the guy she's dating is more *something*

174

than David? Boy, friend, boyfriend. Girl, friend, girlfriend. Maybe it is all about sex.

Louis comes stumbling toward us. His chubbiness seems bulkier, more imposing when he's drunk.

"Baseball is a fag sport," he announces to the assembled infield. From anyone else, this might be an invitation to physical violence, but Louis seems to have been granted a permanent exemption from the rules.

He looks up as if he isn't sure he recognizes me, then smiles so broadly he almost loses his chin. "Mitchell, the old party man. Damn glad you made it." He grabs my non-outstretched hand and pumps it vigorously, then turns back to the baseball players.

"In baseball, you see . . . Christ, what happened to your hair?" He turns back to me and shakes his head sadly. "Damn chemotherapy. Such a tragedy. Anyway, what where we . . . oh, yeah. Fag sports. See, in baseball, all you do is wave around these large shlong substitutes and half the time you strike out anyway. And if you do connect, you're trying to shoot it right out of the park. Pure masturbation. Now soccer, there's a man's sport." He stops to take a long gurgling slurp of his Bud. Louis is the backup goalie and has never, to my knowledge, seen action on the field. He is more like the team mascot.

"You see," he continues, focusing somewhere between David and Glenn, "in soccer it's all about plunking the sperm into the snatch."

Louis smiles at this analogy. There is a moment of silence. He obviously expected some form of response. David shrugs and sips his Diet Coke at the same time, an impressive feat in an odd sort of way. He looks at Louis without smiling.

"And so you're like the second-string diaphragm?" he asks in his usual flat monotone.

Louis breaks into another oversized grin. "Davie boy, that's very, very good—but I prefer to think of myself more as a chastity belt," he answers, holding himself a little more erect before returning to his swaying. "It is my sworn duty to protect the virgin goal from violation by the opposing pricks. And now, I need to find the pisser." And he lumbers off.

I look up at David, who almost smiles. He takes a sip of his Diet Coke. I take a sip of my beer. We seem to be us again.

She touches my arm.
Danielle's materialized.
Hi, hi, how's your head?

Someone touches my arm. I turn around, a little too quickly. Out of nowhere, Danielle has materialized.

"Hi."

"Hi."

"How's your head?"

At first I think she's asking about my haircut, but then

I remember our magical migraine moment last week, which I think is the last time I spoke to her. "I'm okay. I mostly just get them during calculus."

"Bexter will do that to you."

We smile at each other. I'm sure mine looks pasted on. I can feel myself sweating.

"So, how's it going?" she asks.

"Okay."

"Are you having fun?"

Should I be? I shrug.

"Me either."

My mind is racing to come up with something to say. I have no idea why she's suddenly talking to me, but she is. This is intentional, not just a hi, how's it going as she passes by.

"Are you smashed?"

I look at the beer in my hand. "I've been pacing myself," I say, implying that this isn't the only beer I've had this evening.

"Me too, but I don't mind being buzzed, do I? Did you drive?"

"No, I came with—I mean I caught a ride with David."

"Can you drive a stick?"

"No" would be the appropriate answer as both of my family's cars are automatic, but I have driven David's once or twice, not very successfully. Nevertheless, I nod.

"I came with Nicole and she's totally trashed and can I

drive a stick? No way. My car's at her house, and I could give you a ride back to yours."

Okay, so I'm being used for my apparent sobriety, but I don't much care. I wonder if she has any idea what just talking to her does to me.

"Now?"

"Whenever you're ready. I need to scrape Nicole up from wherever she's passed out, but I'm more than ready to call this one done." She sounds tired and frustrated. I remember the look she had coming out of the bathroom, and I wonder what's going on. I miss so much.

"Let me tell David and we'll go."

"You're a sweetheart," she tells me as she begins to work her way back through the room.

David's in the midst of a heated discussion about some umpire. I wait for a pause and tell him a little too loudly that I'm going to drive Danielle and Nicole home, as if this were a regular occurrence. He raises his eyebrows suggestively, an affectation I've never seen from him before.

"Nicole's trashed and Danielle can't drive stick," I explain with a sigh, like this is a real annoyance.

"Catch you later, then," David grunts in his jock voice. He takes a huge swig from his soda. If he's upset, he doesn't show it. I nod and head to the door, where Danielle is waving at me.

I seem to do a lot of nodding.

Nicole drives a Porsche.
I can no longer feel my
fingers: nice car, huh?

Nicole drives a Porsche.

Not that I would have been comfortable wrecking a cheaper vehicle, but the possibility of having an accident in a car that costs as much as a small house terrifies me. I am in an advanced stage of panic. I no longer hear voices. I can no longer feel my fingers.

"Nice car, huh?" Danielle says as she unfolds the tiny backseat and deposits a giggling Nicole into it.

"Great."

Danielle hands me the keys. It takes me an extraordinarily long time to find the right levers to move the seat back, but Danielle and Nicole don't seem to notice. They are discussing the party. Danielle is obviously upset about something or someone. Her quiet angry tone is punctuated by sympathetic bursts of obscenities from Nicole.

"Can you believe he said that to me? Suddenly I'm the slut."

"Asshole!"

"Did I screw around? He's the one who screwed around on me, but somehow this is all my fault."

"Dickhead. What a total dickhead."

Finally, I think I'm ready. Nicole leans over the seat, steadies herself by digging her nails into my right shoulder, and smiles at me. She looks like she is trying to remember who I am, but maybe she's just trying to focus.

"Tricky clutch," she tells me.

Although this does not seem like good news, it actually gives me an excuse for stalling several times before we make it to the first stop sign. Danielle gives me directions, still focused more on relating the details of the evening to Nicole. I concentrate on shifting the gears.

The roads are nearly empty and it's mostly a straight shot down the parkway. I try to relax a little, shifting my posture so I don't look quite so much like a driving plank.

"Why are guys such jerks?" Danielle grumbles. Then she seems to remember I'm there. "Except Mitch. Mitch is a sweetheart."

"He's cute, too," adds Nicole. Suddenly I'm a puppy in the window.

Danielle shifts in her seat so she's facing but not talking to me. "Look, you've embarrassed him." Am I still in this car?

"I don't think I'm the reason he's turning all red. Why don't you go out with Mitch?" Nicole breaks into giggles again.

"Do you want to go out with me, Mitch?"

I'd love to. I'd die to. "I guess so," I say.

"I guess so," Danielle mimics. "Some enthusiasm. Oh, turn here. No, at the light, there we go. Then the first driveway."

The first driveway leads up a small hill, past a gazebo to

a small mansion with columns. The Porsche sputters to a stop behind Danielle's orange BMW.

We haul Nicole out of the car and I hand her the keys. She hugs Danielle good-bye and waves at me, an awkward gesture from a distance of four feet. She then trudges up purposefully to her door, fumbles with the key, waves again, and pushes her way inside.

Danielle shakes her head and I follow her to her car. I want to tell her that I'll just walk home, but I know it would take me hours.

Car lurches and sways,
lost in the high seas in storm.
Thanks for the ride home.

"Where do you live?"

I give her directions and she peels out of the driveway. She is, perhaps, the worst driver I have ever ridden with. We run stop signs, we swerve from shoulder to median, we brake suddenly without apparent cause. She looks as if she's concentrating, but the car lurches and sways as if lost on the high seas in a storm. By the time my house comes into view, I'm hyperventilating.

"Thanks for the ride home," I say as I reach for the door handle.

"Oh, thanks for driving Nicole's car. That was really sweet." Her tone is sincere, but she looks distracted. "Mitch, are you and Amanda, you know, serious?"

I want to ask why she's asking, but I don't. Amanda

and I never dated, barely spoke to each other, and, in all likelihood, will never speak to each other again. I don't explain any of this. I just say, "No."

She smiles again, but it's her practiced one. There's something else happening in her eyes.

"Good night," I say, and this time I get out of the car.

"Night," she responds, and the car jerks to life as the door closes. I watch it swing wildly around the cul-de-sac. She waves as she accelerates past me.

I wave back.

CHAPTER 21

A Catalog of the Basic
Emotions of a
Seventeen-Year-Old Boy

Why would clowns want to juggle sea shells?

In that same health class that suggested note cards as a great way to ask someone out on a date, we were also given a chart showing all the basic emotions. We had to memorize them. There were ten: anger, contempt, disgust, distress, fear, guilt, interest, joy, shame, and surprise. All Clowns Do During Free Get-togethers Is Juggle Sea Shells. I may not be in touch with my feelings, but I can name them.

Guilt

It's Sunday morning, and my house is preternaturally quiet. It's actually almost Sunday afternoon, so I'm guessing that I'm the last one up. There are signs of breakfast: dirty dishes on the table, on the counter, and in the sink. The stove is several inches thick with pancake batter.

I seem to be alone. I scout around for the note. There's

always a note. It would be helpful if the note were always left in the same place, but it never is. I find today's on the living-room sofa.

"Dearest," it begins. I assume that I'm "dearest." Mom calls both of her children "dearest," which makes it a dubious superlative and a non-specific greeting. "Dad is rounding at the hospital. We, the Wells females, went shopping. You were asleep. We knew you wouldn't want to go, so we didn't wake you up. I think that was the right decision. Mom."

Am I supposed to feel grateful or guilty for sleeping in? I choose grateful. I ponder returning to bed.

The phone rings. This is becoming the busiest weekend of my life. I know it's David, and though I'm not sure what I'll say to him about my ride home, I pick up the phone.

"Hi, Mitch."

It's Danielle.

Surprise

There is a pause here where I should be saying hi.

"It's Danielle," says Danielle.

"I know," I say. "Hi."

"Um, I was wondering whether you want to go for a walk or something. It's a nice day and I, um, just wanted to know if you wanted to go for a walk or something."

She's not particularly good at this. She sounds nervous, like she called without knowing what she was going to say. Maybe not everybody uses note cards.

"Sure. I'd love to." *I'd love to*. Hardly casual.

"I'll come pick you up. Are you free now?"

I nod, but I realize she can't hear that, so I manage another "Sure." She says great and we say bye. I hang up the phone.

I'm so confused. I need someone to tell me what's going on. I need advice. I need a shower!

I don't know where Danielle lives, but given the speed at which she drives, I know I don't have much time. I take the quickest shower of my life, dousing myself with shampoo and rinsing off. My skin smells like Head & Shoulders. I spray on my deodorant. The can is almost empty. In a panic, I decide that all of the real ingredients are used up and I'm just spraying the propellant, so I race upstairs and use my dad's roll-on. Then I decide that I've now transferred his sweat to my pits: I run back downstairs and wash my underarms with a soapy washcloth. Feeling calmer about the state of my primary sweat glands, I forgo shaving and run a comb through my tangled hair. My old cowlick has reappeared in the middle of my new haircut, only today it looks like the cow's tongue was covered in glue. Nothing will make that lock of hair lie flat, and I'm debating scissors when the doorbell rings.

Fear

I'm still naked.

Danielle is on my front porch and I'm naked.

I look at myself in the mirror. I'm naked. I don't move. The doorbell rings again.

It takes every ounce of energy for me to yell up the stairs, "Coming." She, no surprise, can't hear that. The doorbell rings again.

I run to the bedroom. There's a pair of underwear, jeans, and a T-shirt lying on the floor. I put them on as fast as I can, and I run up the stairs. I am at the door before I realize that these are the clothes I wore to the party last night. They smell like sweat and cigarette smoke. I am about to run back downstairs, but . . .

"Mitchell?"

She must have heard me coming to the door.

I open the door.

"I need to change clothes," I tell her.

"Hi," she says.

We look at each other. She smiles. It occurs to me that she must smile whenever she's uncomfortable. Like camouflage. She suddenly seems almost human, and I find enough voice to ask, "Would you like to come in?"

Disgust

She smiles again. I realize, belatedly, that she can't come in unless I move out of the doorway. As we walk into the living room, I also realize that our house is a total wreck. Not messy, not unkempt, but demolition rubble. There is stuff everywhere. Jackets and sweaters drape the furniture, dog hair rolls like tumbleweeds across the wood floor. I believe this is the first time I've ever noticed dust.

"I was in the shower," I explain, and then blush. Implying that I was recently naked while she was in close proximity flusters me. "I threw this on because you were . . . here."

She smiles again. I begin to sense that this isn't going well.

"I'll be right back," I tell her and practically run down the stairs.

I put on clean underwear, a fresh pair of jeans, and a polo shirt. It takes me longer than usual to get dressed. Even knowing that I left her upstairs waiting, it takes me forever.

Shame, then anger

When I come back upstairs, Danielle isn't alone.

"When did you get home?"

"Just now. You didn't tell me you were having company," Mom yells from the kitchen, as if the kitchen were far enough away to necessitate yelling. "You could have offered her something to eat."

Unlike a lot of teenagers, I really do love my family. They are, however, the most embarrassing group of misfits ever to walk this planet and, at this moment, I would happily trade them in for a tribe of chimps. Then it gets worse. My dad comes home.

"Hi. Who are you?" he asks, setting down his briefcase. I don't think he means this to sound unfriendly, but it is definitely more CIA than Miss Manners.

"I'm Danielle," she answers, "I'm a friend of Mitch's."

"Since when?"

Dad is always this tactless, it's just how he talks, but today I could strangle him. Danielle looks to me for help, but I can't think of an appropriate response. I'm too busy withering in humiliation.

As Danielle starts to explain that we've been in the same classes all year, Carrie stomps through on the way to the kitchen. We all stop and watch her. She doesn't even acknowledge Danielle's presence on the couch. Carrie opens the refrigerator, pulls out a Diet Pepsi, and returns to her room trailing sullen silence. I get the feeling that she may not like Danielle.

In compensation for Carrie's rudeness and Dad's awkward questions, Mom is fawning. She has placed cookies on a plate and is listing drink options.

"We have to go," I say, loudly and abruptly.

"Go where?" Dad asks.

"Out." The desperation in my voice is obvious, but only Mom picks up on it.

"I think Mitch is trying to tell us to stop harassing his date."

Date? I don't look at Danielle for her reaction, but instead manage a "That would be nice," in what I hope

188

sounds like a lighthearted familial tone and not a pained plea for cessation.

"I was just asking," Dad starts, but Mom drags him toward the hall.

Interest

Danielle and I go for a walk on the Granger easement, near school. I'm only partly there. Or perhaps, the Mitchell I think of myself as isn't there at all. And she's not Danielle, not the Danielle of my fantasy, not the Danielle I see in school. It occurs to me that I've never really heard her talk much before. Her voice is a little squeaky and she moves her arms around as she talks—not just her hands, but the whole length of her arms, from the shoulders to the fingertips. She talks in half questions, which she also answers, requiring very little of me.

"Like, what kind of an idiot volunteers for the prom committee? That would be me. They all want to do 'A Night in Paris' for the theme. I mean, could they come up with a lamer, more overdone theme? Not likely. So I suggested Venice. At least it's another city, right?"

Somehow she segues from the prom to her breakup with Ryan and how she thought she was in love and how she thought everyone really liked her, and something I don't quite follow about how she is tired of being popular and how it makes you shallow, but I wouldn't know about that because I'm not shallow (and, by implication, not popular).

"You're really easy to talk to. Have you always been such a sweetheart? It must be your sister. I wish I had a sister. I'm an only child. Big surprise, huh?"

We sit down. Danielle seems to have run out of steam.

"I'm totally boring and self-obsessed, right?"

"No," I say, trying a little chuckle that might mean "How could you think such a thing?" It's not very convincing. I am not a good chuckler.

"What about you?"

"What about me?"

"Who are you? What do you like to do? I think we have been in the same classes since we were little kids, and I don't know anything about you. How does that happen?"

I think for a moment. The question has caught me off guard. "I don't know," I say.

"You always seem so quiet—but you can tell there's something going on in there somewhere. You always say really smart things in class, not just show-off smart but, like, thoughtful things. You think. Whenever you talk I'm always like, wow—yeah, but I never would have come up with it myself.

"And you watch me. No, don't blush. Not in a bad way, but you do. I think you watch everyone. Every once in a while in English class, I look over and you are watching me and I'm thinking—what is he seeing when he looks at me like that? But then I'm like, no—he's not interested in me, he's just thinking. But maybe I'm wrong?"

With that she leans over and kisses me softly on the mouth.

Surprise, again

I have no idea how to respond. With the exception of those seventh-grade lip bumps, I've never kissed anyone. Danielle smiles and kisses me again, this time not so softly, her lips a little farther apart like maybe she's trying to inhale my lips. When we separate, she looks up at me almost shyly, then more or less attaches herself to my face.

At first I'm a little freaked out by having another person's face so close to mine. I realize that her eyes are closed, and it helps to close mine as well. Otherwise, I'm kissing a cyclops. She presses closer and I let her kiss me, hoping that I'm not supposed to be doing a whole lot on my end. I'm a little overwhelmed by her smell. It's not bad, sort of strawberry or some fruit, but I'm not used to smelling someone so intimately and when that person's practically lying on top of you, it's more noticeable. I try to concentrate. It takes a little while to get used to having someone else's tongue in your mouth, but I think I figure it out and she's not complaining—in fact, she seems to be enjoying herself. I might be too, but it's hard to tell yet.

"This is okay. right?" Danielle asks, pausing for a breath.

Is that a trick question? I manage a sort of nod.

"I'll take that to mean yes," she says, and reattaches.

Joy (if ecstasy counts)

We make out for almost twenty minutes, just kissing and a little bit of rubbing against each other, lying on the grass.

"I should get home," she says. "I still have to do my homework. Does that sound pathetic? Well, it's true. You're a brain. I have to put in the butt time or I'm toast."

The concept of Danielle being a grind doesn't fit my image of her, but she *is* in my honors classes. She's quiet in class, and it hadn't occurred to me that she might be smart.

"Are you okay? I mean with all of this. I know it's moving a little fast, and that I'm a mess . . ."

"I'm okay," I tell her, assuming that ecstatic probably counts as okay. She stands up. Her lips look a little swollen, and she has grass in her hair. My jeans feel overly tight, and I don't dare look down because I'm sure that I still have a visible erection.

"Come on, I really do have to go."

Distress

Thinking about the tightness in my pants only makes it worse. I desperately want to reach in and rearrange my privates. Danielle offers me a hand and I ignore the pain of the squeezing and stand up, praying that it isn't too obvious. She turns to head out of the park and I make what small adjustments I can.

As we walk to the car, Danielle shifts back into manic conversational mode. "I hope my parents didn't get you into too much trouble. They did, didn't they?"

"Your parents?"

"About your English project. My parents complained. I told them about it because I thought it was really funny. Especially the Garden of Eden with all the piles of animal poop—that was hysterical, and I had to go tell my mother about it, didn't I? And of course, my mother would be offended because she's all religious and anything with the devil in it is sure to corrupt her sweet little virginal daughter, because you know I live in a box, right? So I know she called Sorreldrool. I heard that he hauled you out of class to talk to you. He's a little wacked, isn't he? Are you in a lot of trouble?"

Am I in trouble? She lost me at the word "virginal." It's one of those words I can't hear without blushing. "I don't know yet."

"I'm really sorry. I had no idea my parents were going to do that. I mean, I knew they were freaks, but come on."

Actually, I'm sort of impressed that Danielle talks to

her mother about school. It's hard to picture her with parents. She doesn't seem so controlled by anyone.

Danielle kisses me good-bye at her car door. Right in front of my house. A real kiss, deep, the tongue, the whole bit. It feels daring and reckless. I stand in the yard for several minutes after she pulls away. I don't want to go back inside and re-become Mitchell.

Contempt

My parents are sitting in the living room pretending that they aren't waiting for me. I know there is some problem. For starters, Dad is awake and Mom is sitting down.

"She's cute," Dad says as I walk in.

"Thanks," I answer, not sure what I'm taking credit for.

"She seems nice," Mom adds. Her hands are in her lap. My unflappable mother looks flapped. Something about Danielle makes her nervous.

Somehow, in the last hour, our relationship seems to have changed. The couch they sit on is now miles away from where I stand, and they look small and helpless—trapped on their upholstered island. They want to talk, but there is no way I'm talking to my parents about Danielle.

"I've got homework," I say as I disappear down the stairs.

I am not doing homework. I look at the pile of books

on my desk, which may as well have been transported here from the planet Muba. Why does anyone do homework? Everything in my life now feels silly and childish. I can't write in my journal. I don't check my e-mail. I don't call David.

CHAPTER 22

Realities and a Not-Quite Lie or Two

The late Mitchell Wells

I wake up late, not horribly late, but latish. It takes me longer than usual to get myself out of bed. Showering, brushing my teeth, even spraying on my possibly ineffective deodorant seems to take an extraordinarily long time. Even brushing my now-shorn head takes too long. I am in slow motion. It is the opposite of a dream state. Everything feels too real.

Realities:

1) I seem to have a girlfriend. I don't know what I'm supposed to do with a girlfriend. It would be nice if Danielle came with instructions. I am, of course, making the assumption that her tongue in my mouth indicated a changed status—that face sucking means something. That I am now a "boyfriend." But it doesn't feel like one of those

things you can ask about—it feels like I should already know. I don't feel like a boyfriend.

2) I haven't told my best friend (boy and friend, but not boyfriend) that I have a girlfriend. What do I tell David? "Hey, guess what happened to me yesterday?"

When I finally make it to school (Mom drives us; Carrie sits in the back pretending she's being chauffeured and doesn't know either of us), David isn't doing his sort of waiting-for-me-in-the-hall shuffle, but he's never there if I'm really late and I am really late, and sure enough he's already in the classroom—notebook open, pencils ready—when I show up for English with only about thirty seconds to spare. We don't have time to talk and he doesn't seem to be in talking mode anyway. David hasn't seen me since I left the party on Saturday, but he doesn't ask what happened. Maybe he just assumes nothing happened. Normally, that would be a good assumption.

Danielle sits next to me, but she always sits next to me in English, and I'm not sure that anyone else can tell there's something different about the way she is sitting next to me now. I'm not sure I can tell. She takes notes dutifully, writing down everything the substitute writes on the board. This is new. She never took notes before. Maybe now that she is dating a nerd, she feels like she needs to look more studious.

Nothing else seems different. Ms. Chimneystack talks, mainly to the blackboard, but about the book. She occasionally asks a question and Mariel answers it. This arrangement works well for both of them, and the rest of us are happy with it too. Danielle fills three pages of her notebook, as if she's been taking dictation. I've spent the entire period watching her take notes.

English ends and we walk out, pretty much like we have done all year. But this time, there is a moment in the hallway, when there are three of us standing there rather than two. Then Danielle says, "French," because that's her next class, and I say, "Calculus," which is what David and I both have next, and she smiles a see you later and we all go off to class.

We have said two words, neither very revealing, but it is enough to show that something has changed.

David doesn't say a word.

After calculus, David goes to German and I have a free. I don't know what Danielle has, so I hang out a little at her locker, trying to pull off David's trick of not looking like I'm hanging out at someone's locker. I don't manage it as well, and after a few minutes of pacing between the J. P. Gilley water fountain, my own locker, and the space in front of Danielle's, I give up and go to the library. I meet David again at history and I have a small attack of paranoid guilt that someone else has told him about Danielle and me, but all he does is ask me a question about our chemistry assignment (the syllabus said chapter 10, pages 116–142 but the actual chapter 10 goes on to 146 and it wasn't clear whether we had to read those four pages—I thought we probably should), and I assume he hasn't heard, because I feel that if he had, he'd say something about it, although for the life of me I can't figure out what I'd expect him to say.

◉ ◉ ◉

Lunch is next. David is carrying his in his backpack (he only returns to his locker twice a day as a rule) but I never think ahead, so we head off separately. I find Danielle leaning on my locker, not looking relaxed and definitely waiting for me. I consider kissing her, just a friendly peck on the mouth the way my parents often do, but they have years of practice in this protocol, so instead I stand a safe distance away and say hi in what I'm hoping is a calm tone but I suspect is more of a scared squeak. Danielle isn't smiling.

"Look," she says. I look down at the carpet because that's where she is looking, but there isn't anything there to see. "I have a meeting during activity. Stupid prom stuff. So I'll see you at lunch, okay?"

"I have lunch now."

"You have early lunch?" Danielle has obviously never noticed my absence from junior lunch.

"Because of Wallman."

"Then maybe between?"

I nod. Danielle pushes herself off the locker, which brings her almost into kissing range, but she doesn't look like she wants me to kiss her and I don't try. Maybe we haven't been together long enough for public kissing. She does her less-than-comfortable-with-the-situation smile and leaves me standing there. I don't watch her walk down the hall.

In order to open my locker I need to step forward a grand total of about three steps, but it takes all of my willpower to make it there. My books have gained several pounds apiece, and my muscles strain to lift them into my locker. I know David is waiting for me at lunch.

Somehow unpredictably predictable

David is waiting for me at lunch.

"How's married life?" he asks as we sit down, breaking off half of his roast beef sandwich for me. This is an unusual gesture. I think I prefer having to beg.

"So you heard?"

"Everybody's talking about it. Nobody has a good explanation for why she's dating a loser like you."

David's use of the term "loser" is a factual classification, not an insult. I don't have a good explanation for it either. I keep scanning his face for some sort of reaction. He is still there, still David, his chips on the napkin in front of him next to his shiny red apple. How widespread does this gossip have to be if David knows?

"It's a little weird," I admit. "I keep wondering if I just dreamed the whole thing."

David shrugs at this. I try to take in what it might mean if *everyone* is talking about it. As if in answer, Louis appears.

"So," he says as he plops into the chair next to me.

"Hello, Louis," David says evenly. "Please, pull up a chair."

Louis ignores this sarcasm, which is easy to do since, in typical David delivery, it lacks anything approximating a sarcastic tone. Instead he looks up brightly and addresses David in a voice full of unrelenting cheer. "It's so nice to see that you're handling your squeeze double-dipping with little D. Very bigamist of you."

David's reaction is hard to read. My face must show nothing but confusion as I try to translate.

"Quite a shocker," Louis continues as he reaches over and helps himself to David's potato chips. "I had you two pegged for the queen and the queen of the prom. I mean, you two have been dating for—what?—almost a year now? So, Mitch, are you trading in the old stroke and swallow for a little bearded clam action?"

David looks up at me, and we take too long to respond. Louis turns to face David full on.

"Don't look so surprised, closet boy. Mitch here could go either way, even with that haircut, but you've never been on the straight and narrow." Over the goofy smile, Louis's eyes are still and observant. He may have been just prospecting, but he knows he has hit ore. He's not about to let up.

"You can tell me," he mock-whispers.

"You're an asshole, Louis," David says, but his voice is more serious than it should be.

"True but irrelevant, Suckmaster Flash. You might as well have it tattooed on your cheeks, either end. You can't even lie about it. Just try. Look me in the eye and tell me that you aren't gay."

Louis is right; I've never known David to lie. I am beginning to visibly panic, but David folds his napkin calmly and pockets his apple. He then looks Louis straight in the eye and says, convincingly, "We aren't gay."

He says the words without inflection, but I can hear the emphasis on the pronoun.

Lately I seem to be more and more confused by pronouns

After Louis leaves, David and I don't discuss what happened. Maybe nothing happened—Louis picks on everybody, and his questioning of David might just have been his abuse du jour. But as I walk back to wait for Danielle outside the Forrest Klimer Multipurpose Conference Room, I have an attack of the uneasies.

Danielle emerges from her committee meeting looking emotionally bruised.

"I hate everyone who goes to this school," she announces to me as I walk her to her lunch. So far, our relationship has consisted of one visit to a park, a conversation at my locker, and two walks in the hallway. Except for the kissing part, I could be replaced by a good spaniel. "I don't hate you," she adds as an afterthought.

"What about Nicole? I thought you two were still . . ."

"Don't even breathe the bitch's name. She told Ryan everything I said about him. She went and told Ryan what I said. Can you fucking believe that? I think he's screwing her too."

As the apparent new boyfriend, I am a little put off by her concern about what Ryan is doing. I'm not sure how to voice my objections, and so instead I take an unusually avid interest in my feet, which are plodding along in Danielle's wake. I have been staring at Danielle every chance I got for years, and now I'm afraid to look at her.

Danielle stops suddenly and I almost bump into her. She faces me and tries to find my eyes, which involves a little bending. Finally I look up. "Are we doing all right?" she asks.

I nod. She isn't, I'm not, but I'm still hoping *we* are.

Her eyes search my face. I'm not sure what she's looking for. "Are you taking me to the prom?" she asks. It's more of a challenge than a question.

"Do you want to go to the prom with me?" It's a question, not an invitation.

"Okay. I just needed to know. Are we double-dating with David? Does David have a date?"

"M.C."

"He's dating Marie Claire. That's cute. I didn't know that."

"Mary Clarissa. They're just going to the prom together."

"He should date her."

Punctuation matters

I say good-bye to Danielle at the cafeteria door, wondering, but not asking, who she will sit with. I decide that I need to go to my locker before heading over to the film lab.

"Is it true?" M.C. is standing between me and my locker.

"What?"

"Carrie said she was at your house yesterday. Are you really dating Danielle?"

There are at least three good responses to this question. I could ask why she cares, I could ask why it is any of her business, or I could tell her that I'm allowed to date whoever I want to, but all I say is "Yes."

M.C. looks at me like she's not quite sure who I am. "Wow," she says.

We stand in the hall and stare at each other until I am totally uncomfortable. M.C. seems frozen in place. I have never known her to be at a loss for words, but here she is standing in front of me like she wants to ask me something but can't get it out. I've known her for so long, but the person opposite me in the hallway isn't the seven-year-old who used to steal my Transformers so they could date her Barbies or the twelve-year-old who used to screech during sleepovers with Carrie.

"Are we still going to double-date for the prom?" I ask her.

"Do you still want to go with me—and David?"

"Why wouldn't I?"

"Then sure, if David is still taking me."

"I think he is."

M.C. nods, but doesn't move. "Could you ask him?"

"I can do that. Not a problem."

M.C. smiles and regains her animation. "Call me tonight. Please?" Only the "please" has a question mark attached. I tell her I will.

Wallman weighs in

"Mitchell, could we talk for a moment?"

I look up from the little lump of Plasticine that I am trying my best to attach to a round-shaped armature. I was hoping for an armadillo, but this thing is most likely on its way to becoming a slug. Wallman is standing beside me fidgeting and chewing on his beard.

"Sure," I say.

"Let's step outside."

I follow him out of the troll cave, half expecting he will evaporate or explode when he steps through the door. We stand in the hallway, and he does look a little different in the fluorescent light. His jeans and sweater, which are formless in the dim lab, are baggy but reasonable out here. There are no visible stains anywhere. His face is lined and furrowed in places. He is older than I thought, but mostly he looks like a teacher.

"I understand that you have been asked to appear before the Judicial Board."

"Yes."

"Because of the film you turned in for your English assignment."

I nod. My first reaction is relief. At least Wallman isn't asking me about Danielle. It kind of sucks when you're relieved to be discussing your own possible expulsion.

"Was it because you had made it originally for this class? Did Curtis . . . Mr. Curtis consider that cheating?"

"Um . . . no. That never came up. It was because someone in the class, or someone's parents, thought it was . . . um . . . offensive. To their religion."

"You're kidding."

"No."

Wallman looks confused. He scratches at his beard. "I was going to go talk to Sorrelson, if you wanted me to, to tell him that I thought it was okay to use the film for your English class. I could still talk to him if you want me to. Would it help if I told him that I approved the content? You should probably know that we . . ." He scratches his beard again. He's trying to be diplomatic, something he never feels the need to do inside his class-room. "We don't see eye to eye." He sighs, then gives up trying to impersonate an actual member of the faculty. "He's an ass, but you've probably noticed that. But if you want me to . . ."

This is not the Wallman I know. He looks smaller, almost human. He is volunteering to help because he feels responsible in some way, or he likes me, or maybe just because he's a nice guy, but he clearly wants me to say no. Of the two of us in this hallway, I'm feeling like the only adult.

"Thank you," I tell him as sincerely as I can. "I think it will be fine. But I appreciate the offer. I really do."

He seems relieved.

"Maybe we could skip the religious imagery in your next project," Wallman suggests, but the joke feels a little flat. I go with it anyway.

"Don't worry, only sex and violence."

"Good," he says, smiling and fidgeting. He's had enough of the outside world and needs to return to the gloomy comfort of the lab.

When I get back to our construction table, David is taking a turn trying to armadilize the slug. He asks what Wallman wanted. It isn't until I am halfway through telling David what happened that I realize Wallman had just volunteered to lie to his boss on my behalf. I wonder what his relationship with the administration and the rest of the faculty is like. Does he have friends here? I have a sudden awful vision of the world as just a much bigger version of high school, where adults still have to worry about being popular and whether someone in charge has it in for you. Please don't let that be true.

CHAPTER 23

The Day the World Changed
(Some Observations About Breasts)

"We are a race of tit men . . ." —Henry David
Thoreau

The world doesn't change slowly. It changes all at once. I can remember, almost to the minute, the day we became teenagers. It was somewhere around 2:20 on a Thursday afternoon in the spring of seventh grade, either the last week of March or the first week of April.

We were sitting in art class and drawing Rebecca Kessler. We each took turns being models. Fully clothed, of course; we were only in seventh grade. I was doing my best to draw something that might qualify as vaguely humanoid. Everyone else was talking about a party that had been thrown by someone in the eighth grade, which some of the girls had been invited to—somebody's house had been TP'd or something. I was not startled by the acts of juvenile delinquency. Something more important had transpired. There were now parties to which not all of us had been invited.

We were a small class. Maybe forty kids in the whole

grade at that point. Everyone went to the parties. Parties were controlled by the Mothers. Mothers sent in valentines for everyone in the class and baked cupcakes on birthdays and always insisted that everybody be invited to parties. Sometimes a party might be all guys or all girls, but the Mothers would never sanction exclusion based on any criteria other than gender. Now we were entering a world where our social lives were no longer controlled by our mothers. This new world was a much more frightening place. The pecking order would now be public, our self-esteem more tendentious, our fate more directly in the hands of our classmates. It would be harder to pretend that we were cool. Now there would be choosing, and some of us would form the ranks of the unchosen.

If this had been the only thing that changed that day, I probably could have learned to deal with it. But there was more. During that conversation, Ryan—who, by the way, was the only boy from our class who'd gone to that party—had been concentrating on drawing Rebecca. Now, by seventh grade, Rebecca had already become a junior goddess. Shoulder-length blond hair held back with a hairband, big blue eyes, always tan. She had delicate features but she was never prissy. She could wear a dress and look sweet, but she was athletic and competitive and would regularly kick butt on the soccer field.

Rebecca sat on the stool, her bare legs dangling from a short but appropriate skirt. Her knit jersey was neatly tucked in, emphasizing her rapidly developing body. It seemed to be developing at an almost visible pace. She had tits and we knew it. I never said a word about them, but all the rest of that year the boys who knew what French kissing actually meant and talked about meeting girls at parties, girls from other schools where all sorts of things happened all the time—held lengthy discourses about Rebecca's breasts. No one claimed to have touched them. Rebecca was not an object of gossip, only admiration.

And not just ours. By the end of the year, Rebecca was dating a sophomore, and as an eighth grader she went to the junior/senior prom. Then her mom packed her off to some all-girls boarding school and we never heard from her again.

But that day, as she sat modeling for us, the world changed. We became different. I can trace it to a single moment. While I was standing there drawing, unsuccessfully trying to wrestle my pencil into at least allowing me to keep her eyes on separate sides of her nose, Ryan drew a simple line sketch. Nothing fancy, just straightforward, clean lines, proper proportions, profile. Then he did something that the rest of us wouldn't have dared to do. In one simple curved line, he drew what he saw. His profile of the seated Rebecca included her breast.

When the teacher held up Ryan's sketch, Louis laughed out loud. The rest of us stared mutely, unsure of how we were supposed to react. Rebecca blushed, but she was a goddess; she did not burst into tears. Ms. Winslow then complimented Ryan on the drawing. She did not make direct reference to the breast, but she obviously thought the picture had been properly done. I did not give Rebecca breasts in my sketch. Yet somehow, with that line, we all crossed some sort of boundary.

◉ ◉ ◉

Danielle's shirt has an awful lot of buttons. Little teeny buttons. It ends just above midriff and the skin underneath is pale and less firm than it looks. I hadn't intended to place my hand on that exposed flesh, but as she moves toward me on the couch I have to hold her somewhere for balance and, without thinking, I place my hand on her side. I am touching her skin. Not an arm that I see every day, but a part of her body that is usually covered by clothing. She doesn't seem to mind; in fact, she leans into me more. I haven't figured out what to do with my other hand yet, so I leave it by my side, which probably looks awkward, but I know she can't see it and I don't think we would be doing this at all if we had an audience.

We are on the couch in her living room. Her parents aren't home and Danielle says we have about half an hour, which I interpret to mean that we can make out on the couch but we aren't going to take off our clothes and jump into bed, which is in fact a relief to me. Although I've certainly imagined sex, I haven't imagined that we would actually be having it; I think I'd want to have talked about it first. But since even kissing is new for me, I am more than happy to follow her lead. Bodies, I quickly learn, take a little adjusting to get into kissing position, and none of this comes naturally for me.

So my hand is on her side, and as she shifts, I realize that there are only a few inches between that location and the bottom of her breasts. There is enough room beneath her shirt for my hand. So do I ask? How would I phrase it? "May I touch your breasts?" Should I call them "breasts" or is that too clinical? What about "May I touch you?" Does the word "may" make me sound too formal?

Danielle has stopped kissing me and I realize that I must have gotten distracted. I blush. Now that she has my attention again, she moves a little more into my lap, her arms around my neck. She is a little heavier than I imagined she'd be, but I'm not uncomfortable.

She raises her face toward mine. My left hand is on her back, but my right is sort of in her lap. As I try to replace it on her side I realize that in her new position, my hand is on the side of her left breast. I rest it there tentatively. She doesn't say anything, so I move my hand a little farther. I wait for a reaction.

I get one. She sits up straighter and slips her shirt off over her head. I stare at her.

"Were you thinking you'd have to undo all those little buttons? They're just for show."

I hadn't actually gotten as far as the buttons, but I smile anyway. She doesn't make any motion signaling that she wants me to take off the bra, so I place my hand on the embroidered cup, and she leans into me. I'm not sure what I expected, but the material feels almost spongy. The breasts beneath the material are firmer than I imagined. I try to be gentle, not squeezing but sort of massaging. She giggles a little, but doesn't seem upset. As she leans in to kiss me again, a car goes by.

"Oh my God, your parents."

"We'll hear the garage door open. I can get my shirt on pretty quickly. Don't worry."

I worry, but not enough to ask her to put her shirt back on.

CHAPTER 24

Life Is Different

Life is different

I'm a little late for history and Louis has taken my regular seat, but I'm handling it well. From across the room I watch David and Mariel discuss the prom. They are both laughing. Mariel isn't going to the prom—she's not interested. She and Libby and a couple of other people are headed up to somebody's lake house for the weekend. She thinks it's all a little too silly. Maybe I do too.

Mariel is making a joke about rented pants that has David in hysterics. I haven't seen David laugh since I threw an egg roll at him. Even then, he wasn't laughing like this. Why aren't we funny anymore?

Life is different

"I'm supposed to ask you whether you and I are still taking M.C. and Danielle to the prom."

David listens closely to my very carefully worded question.

"You're supposed to ask me, but you're not asking me?"

"No, I guess I'm actually asking. M.C. wasn't sure, but I was pretty sure, but maybe I shouldn't be. Do we have a reservation?"

"I do, but I'm guessing it isn't that hard to change it from two to four. You may have to stand the whole meal and eat table scraps."

"I'm used to that," I tell him. He looks up at me, sighs loudly, and breaks the remainder of his sandwich in half.

"Don't you have a girlfriend now who can feed you?"

Life is different

"I talked to David, and we are double-dating for the prom. He called the restaurant and everything is set. Hello?"

The person who answered the phone had said she was M.C., but now the line is strangely silent.

"M.C.?"

"I'm here."

"You asked me to ask David, then call you. I asked David, and now I'm calling you."

"I know."

"So the answer is yes."

"I know. David already told me."

M.C. sounds teed off. I've heard what she sounds like when she's angry at her parents, at teachers, at her brothers, at Carrie, and at any number of girls from her class, but I've never heard her be angry at me.

"What did I do wrong?"

"Did you tell Louis that I had a great ass?"

"No," I say, immediately offended that she would think I'd say that. "I mean, it's not that I don't think you . . . I mean, I . . . but I didn't . . . I would never . . . not to Louis."

"He said that you guys were talking and that you said I had a great ass."

"I don't think I said that." But maybe I did, sort of. At least I agreed when he said it.

"I don't appreciate you going around talking about me like I'm just walking body parts. I thought we were friends."

"I do not go around talking about you that way." I really don't. Except maybe that once.

"Then why did he say you did? Why would he make that up?"

Because he's a jerk—although that's not the word he would use. "Here's what happened, and you have to believe me. Louis gave me a ride home and he was talking about a bunch of stuff and he made a comment about your . . . ass and what was I supposed to say—no, she has an ugly ass? Should I have slugged him for suggesting you might be attractive? It wasn't a nice way of saying it, but it is what he meant. Why were you talking to Louis anyway?"

"I wasn't trying to talk to him. He was asking me about David and you and then he said that, and, I don't know, I felt upset because I had this picture in my head of you guys sitting around rating me and how my ass compares with Natalie's or Danielle's or somebody's, and I know guys do that, but you're my friend, aren't you?"

"I thought so."

"Me too." She is thawing. I can hear it in her voice. "Louis is a jerk," she adds.

"Yes."

"He considers you one of his best friends."

Really? I spend a lot of time with Louis, mostly in small groups. Occasionally he, David, and I have gone somewhere together, though I don't remember ever inviting him directly. If you aren't required to like your friends, I guess someone looking at our lives could call us friends.

"How about I promise never to mention your ass again, to him or anyone, no matter how great it is? Are we friends again?"

"What about my boobs?"

I promise not to mention those either, then I offer ice cream. She takes a rain check, she's got to babysit, but her answer, she tells me, is definitely yes. There is a pause. Then she asks me if I think Danielle would mind. I tell her I'm pretty sure that I'm allowed to eat ice cream with friends, even the ones with great asses.

"You know," she says seriously, "things felt a lot more simple a few weeks ago."

"I know. Trust me, I know."

Life is different

It is a beautiful spring day and Danielle informs me that she wants a picnic dinner. In theory, we were on our way home to work on our homework. Ms. Chimneystack had reminded us yesterday that we still had to do the essays on the syllabus even if Curtis was on leave, and this time there is no way I'm doing anything other than a perfectly normal, boring, five-paragraph essay. But now Danielle wants a picnic, and at this moment that seems much more pressing than passing English. We stop at the 7-Eleven for single-serving pecan pies, the kind in the little tin plates, Pringles, and Dr Peppers. She chooses these items with an intensity that borders on obsession. My suggestion of the barbecue-flavored Pringles is flatly rejected, but I am allowed to add a Heath bar for dessert. We park by the pond at the Granger easement and she pulls a blanket from her trunk, which we spread out in a spot without too much goose poop. Danielle takes off her shoes. For a while we do nothing but eat potato chips and enjoy the fading sunshine.

"It feels like being away," she says, smiling a real smile. "You okay?"

It's her favorite question. Danielle seems to need con-firmation that things are going well. Maybe she doesn't trust her sense of reality. Maybe she just isn't too trusting.

"I think so. Do you think so?"

"Maybe." She gives a small shrug, like she just thought

of something that she wishes she hadn't. "None of your friends like me, do they?"

I don't disagree. How would I answer that?

"I'm sure they think that I'm using you because I need to make Ryan jealous or I need a date to the prom or I'm just a slut who needs to have a male. Why doesn't that piss you off? Why is it so hard to believe that I might actually like being around you?"

Because I'm not a Ryan. I'm Mitchell Wells—pretty shy, a little nerdy, not a bad guy, but hardly someone people are waiting in line for. I don't cause swoons. Maybe I'm not so trusting either.

"Are we friends?" she asks.

"I think so."

"Because if we aren't friends, then it doesn't mean anything."

"I'd like to be friends," I tell her, wondering what she means by the word.

"Me too," she says, looking down at the grass. Her voice becomes very quiet, as if she's telling the grass a secret that she isn't so sure she wants me to hear. "You know, at the party, at Josh's party the other night when you gave Nicole a ride home, it was such a shitty night, and I was just so totally—I don't know, I felt completely alone. I was ready to leave Nicole there, and maybe I should have, but I was still hoping maybe I had one friend. And then I walked into the living room and saw you and I touched your arm and you were the first person to look me in the eyes all night. And when you looked away, it wasn't because you were thinking something horrible about me. You were really cute. Shy. But there is something about your eyes. I felt like I could trust you."

I watch her stretch out her bare feet and she snuggles down next to me, which almost knocks me over, but I regain my balance and slide my arm around her and she curls up with her head on my shoulder and her legs across mine. Propped against the hillside, we watch the sunset, and for a moment I have a glimpse of the bubble that usually surrounds me—the space that almost no one enters. Seventeen-year-old guys don't get touched a lot. Parents hug. There are high fives and handshakes. People bump into you by accident. But Danielle doesn't see the bubble. She reaches in and touches my face with her fingertips. She leans her head on my shoulder. She touches me like she needs reassurance that I'm solid, that I'm really there.

Later, when we finally leave the park and are standing kissing by her car, she slides her hand down my back and under the curve of my butt. It isn't a grope, but it isn't a pat. I have had my hands on her backside already, but I've never had someone touch me that way. Her mouth tastes like chocolate and toffee. She tells me she wants to be friends, first and foremost. She doesn't know anyone who listens to her like I do. She needs me. She isn't sure what she would have done without me. It's all confusing, she says, she's only dated one other person her whole life—someone she'll admit she still is "messed up" over and she's not sure where this is going and she doesn't want to get hurt and she doesn't want to hurt me and we talked on that blanket for two hours and yet nothing she said makes any sense to me because I can feel the pulse in her neck when I kiss it and I can feel her chest against mine and all I want to do is be with her.

CHAPTER 25

Words I Thought Were English

A vocabulary of Danielle

Lunch is almost over. David is at an away game and I am avoiding everyone else I know, so I eat quietly on the wall outside the auditorium. As a lunch spot it isn't wonderful—there's a great view of the parking lot—but it has the advantage of not being a place where anyone else ever goes. I have less than a week until my appearance before the Judicial Board. I should be preparing some kind of defense. Instead, I'm sitting here trying to relearn the English language.

Yesterday, Danielle and I agreed to meet and "study" together in the library. Even though she said it in what sounded like a seductive voice, I'm guessing that she means we're really going to be busy memorizing the periodic table for our chemistry test. Still, it is something.

Danielle says we have to "take it slow." I'd like a timer. Do I call her every night? Every other night?

Danielle tells me she's just being "cautious." She has to protect herself from getting hurt again. It is so hard to imagine how I could hurt her, short of forgetting what I was doing and biting her tongue. She doesn't seem vulnerable around me. I hear her say it, but no matter how I try, I cannot see myself as a heartbreaker. She keeps telling me she's a "mess," but she's the most put-together mess I've ever seen. She really likes me, she says, but she's not ready to jump into something "serious." So we aren't serious. What does a not-serious relationship mean? Are we just friends who kiss? Is "serious" a code word for sex?

Define "friend"

Books from the locker, a drink from the water fountain, and I turn the corner to find Amanda. Amanda is standing in the hall. Amanda is standing in the hall by the entrance to the library where I am supposed to be meeting Danielle. By herself. Amanda is short, maybe five-one if her shoes have thick soles, but standing in front of the library she fills the whole hallway. There is no way around her. I'm not sure she's seen me yet, so I retreat back toward my locker. The library is one side of the square around the lunchroom, so if I do the whole circuit I will approach it from the other side. With luck, she'll be gone by then. I check my watch. The period hasn't started yet. Surely she has a class to go to. Cornering me can't be worth a detention. I cut past the freshman lockers, so I can duck into the bathroom if she follows me.

224

But how do I know if she is following me unless I look back? I put my hand on the bathroom door, which puts me in profile so that my glance back won't be too obvious. I glance back. No Amanda.

The bathroom door opens and I nearly fall in. To Ryan. Ryan is standing in the entrance to the bathroom. He doesn't move to let me enter.

I have this very clear image from some nature film I saw that had these two male rams facing off in single combat. They stood, muscles taut, daring the other to move first, the mountain air thick with testosterone and sweat. The tension was tremendous, waiting for the violent and inevitable crash of the horns as the mighty animals hurled themselves at each other. That's not us.

"Oops," is my macho response to the situation. I follow with an "Excuse me" and he lets me pass. I have to at least pretend I was planning to go in, why else would my hand be on the door?

◎   ◎   ◎

After an appropriate amount of time, I leave the bathroom and finish the circuit to the library. Amanda is gone. I don't see Danielle yet, so I find a little table off to one side, near the window and . . .

"Hi, Mitchell." Amanda slides into the chair across from me. I want to tell her it is already taken. "I think you've been avoiding me," she says in a soft voice.

Avoiding, hiding, actively running away from. "No," I

tell her as confidently as I can, given that both of us know I'm lying. She is half smiling, like she's thinking of something pleasant and far away. It's a confusing sort of smile. An angry smile.

"I heard you're taking Danielle to the prom," she says with a casual vehemence.

"Yeah, um . . . well, we've started, sort of . . . seeing each other." That's honest. We might be slow and unserious, but it still counts.

"I know. I heard." Meaning, you didn't tell me yourself.

"Do you have a free this period?"

"When were you going to tell me?"

"Because you are really late for your class."

"*Were* you going to tell me?"

I don't know. "Yes," I tell her. "Yes, I was. Next time we bumped into each other." Which would have been never if I could have helped it.

"It would have been nice if I could have heard it directly from you," she says, losing the smile from her anger.

"I'm sorry."

"Thanks, because I think you mean that. Can we talk?"

I so want to say no.

"I know that it isn't going to come out right and I know I don't have any right to say this, but I consider us friends and I feel like someone has to tell you."

Have I contracted some disease? Is there something stuck in my teeth? What is she talking about?

"Mitchell, I'm worried about you. I know you like Danielle and I'm sure she's a really great person, but everybody knows she uses people. Don't you think it's a little strange that she is suddenly in love with you? What, has she not noticed that you've been in her class since first grade? And now, just when no one else will even speak to her after what she did to Ryan, this lightning bolt hits her that you're the one? You're cute, Mitchell, but you're hardly her type. She's got to be desperate. That sounds harsh, but I just think you should know that's what people are saying. And if it were me, I'd want someone to tell me if everyone thought I was being used, you know."

Amanda stops short and looks up. I can tell from her facial expression who is crossing the library toward us.

"I've got to go—I'm late for class. I'm just trying to be a good friend, Mitchell, really."

Really?

I'm sure Danielle saw Amanda fleeing the library, but all she says when she joins me is, "There you are, buddy." I feel her hand on the back of my head before she speaks. Danielle likes to touch. My hair, my arm, a hand resting on my shoulder. If I am being used, what am I being used for? Other than a date for the prom, it's hard to see what Danielle gains from dating me.

While I'm busy enjoying the hair stroking, a less welcome face slides into view.

"Buddy? Wow, that's so . . . saccharine. It's cute. If

you're going to emasculate the poor guy, at least call him 'puppy' or 'sweetie' or something."

"Louis?"

"Yes, Danielle."

"Go away."

"Can't," Louis says as he plops his bulk into the chair Amanda just vacated. "I need to talk to my little buddy here."

"Not now, Louis."

"Please go away," Danielle repeats.

"No, no—this is for your own good. You guys can play library later. If you can keep your hands out of her indices for a few minutes, I have something serious to tell you." He turns to Danielle. "You know, from what I know of Mitchell, yours may be the first pair of female lips he's ever sucked on. Is he a fast learner? Is he figuring out what to do yet or is it like sticking your tongue into an open spigot?" Danielle rolls her eyes, sits next to me, and opens her chemistry book. Nothing will deter Louis.

"I just got the word. Sorrelson is sending you to the J-Board. Day in court. Very interesting. Passing the buck, letting the juvies decide your fate. Now usually I'm the hanging judge type . . ."

"How did you even get on the Judicial Board?"

Louis looks offended. "Elected by my peers, and lucky for you I was too, because I am one of the few people who truly gets it. It's a freedom of expression thing. First

Amendment. Tits as art. Someone has to take a stand, and I'm proud of you, my son. Now, usually I recommend groveling. That goes down well with the J-Board. But a brave man like yourself should take on the establishment. Give it to the man. Consequences be damned, liberty or death. We are with you, brother. Long live the revolution!"

Louis stands, raises his fist in solidarity, and finally leaves. Danielle looks at me.

"J-Board?"

"Yeah. Next week."

"I could kill my parents." She looks genuinely upset. We spend the rest of the period writing out flash cards, Danielle's left elbow resting on my right arm as I whisper chemical elements to her softly. I decide being a nerd isn't such a horrible thing.

Who is "we"?

It is Friday. Usually on Fridays David and I go to a movie. Or hang out and watch TV. Sometimes we go to a party or a game. But it's always been easy. We did *something*. Now there's Danielle. We haven't talked about what happens now.

◉　◎　◎

First attempt to talk to David:

Me: It's Friday.

David: I know.

◎　◎　◎

First attempt to talk to Danielle:

Me: About tonight . . .

Danielle: I don't know what you were thinking, but I was thinking maybe about eight. Could I be ready at eight? Maybe, but I could try because then we could have a little time before going over to Emily's. Don't look that way. It isn't a party, just a couple of people, and Emily is one of the few people who has been relatively nice to me since everything happened.

◎　◎　◎

Second attempt to talk to David:

Me: Danielle said something about Emily having a party tonight. Not a *party* party, just a few people.

David: I don't know. What about a movie?

◎　◎　◎

Second attempt to talk to Danielle:

Me: I was talking to David. Just checking in about tonight.

Danielle: Is he coming to Emily's?

Me: I don't think so.

Danielle: That's good. I wasn't supposed to be telling lots of people about it. She gets all wiggy about her house when her parents are gone and she doesn't want a lot of gatecrashers.

One, maybe two, or possibly three of us are in denial. In a bizarre turn of events, I have too much to do on a Friday night. I consider faking a stomach virus. Instead I call David when I get home.

"Hello."

"Hi, David, it's Mitchell."

"I know."

"Danielle really wants to go to Emily's tonight."

"And you want to go with her."

It would be helpful to know if that is a question or a statement.

"No, but I think I maybe should."

"Okay. What time is the party?"

"I don't know. It's more just a few people getting together."

"Call me back."

I call Danielle.

"Hi, guy."

"David wants to go to the party."

"I thought you said he wanted to go to a movie."

"He did, but with me."

"Can't he go with someone else?"

"I don't know."

We all go to Emily's. David meets us there. I stand uncomfortably between him and Danielle while they talk to different people but never each other. Danielle insists it's not a party, but it's a lot like all the parties I go to except I'm here with two people, neither one of whom is

231

spending much time talking with me. David is also drinking. He's decided he likes beer, he tells me in the same assured way he defended his lack of taste for it in the past. All told, he drinks about three beers, which I tell myself isn't enough to worry about. When it gets late, I leave with Danielle. David half smiles a good-bye.

CHAPTER 26

More Words I Thought Were English

An herbaceous, biennial, and dicotyledonous flowering plant of the family Brassicaceae (or Cruciferae), sometimes decorative but often used in dishes such as coleslaw—but that's not what's for dinner

Doesn't one of you have a teacher named Al Curtis?" Dad asks as he walks into the house. None of us except Hubert are standing in the hallway, so the question is more or less addressed to the dog. The bipedal members of the family are all sitting in the kitchen.

"I do, or did," I stammer from my perch at the breakfast bar.

"Nice guy." At first I assume this is a question, but the inflection is wrong. Dad is making a statement. Where has he met Curtis?

Dad helps himself to coffee from the pot that has been sitting cold since breakfast. It can't be tasty at this point, but he drains his mug and refills it. "What's for dinner?"

he asks. We all look down at our plates. None of us is quite sure what to call it.

"Brown stuff," Carrie volunteers.

"It's sort of a tofu stir-fry," my mother explains. When the one who cooks it uses a term like "sort of," it's a bad sign.

Dad doesn't seem to be following up on his remark about Curtis. He takes down a plate and tops two spoonfuls of rice with a token sampling of the stir-fry. He then takes the vacant stool beside Carrie at the breakfast bar and begins shoveling the contents of his plate into his mouth, chewing quickly in the interval when his fork travels to and from the plate. Finally I ask, "Where did you meet Curtis?"

"At the hospital," he replies without stopping the food intake process. Rice and globs of brown sauce dribble back onto his plate.

"Is he sick?"

Dad shakes his head. He takes a sip from his coffee cup and gurgles, "His mom."

It's not exactly a surprise that Curtis has a mother, but somehow it feels wrong to think of him as somebody's son. I'm somebody's son.

"What's wrong with her?"

Dad, in a rare display of manners, actually stops chewing. "She presented a couple of weeks ago with an M.I. with q's and flipped t's. Her discharge stress test showed some ischemia, so we upped her beta blocker, but she came back with angina, some atrial fibrillation, and she had a cabbage."

Carrie and I stare at him blankly.

"You fed her cabbage?" Carrie asks, finally.

I'm glad she asked. I was wondering too.

"Bypass surgery. She had a heart attack and CABG is bypass surgery," Mom explains. She speaks Cardiothoracic Surgospeak more fluently than the rest of us.

Dad nods and returns his attention to inhaling his food. After a few more mouthfuls he pauses for another gulp of coffee and adds, "She had some complications. Al's been there the whole time. Nice guy. He and his fiancée, nice young woman, kind of tall, they've been taking shifts with her, reading to her, holding her hand. Al tried to go back to work but he said he didn't make it all the way through his class and the school gave him leave. Good son. Nice family—well, I think I'll have more. Anyone else want seconds?"

I decline, planning to sneak down later and find something more readily identifiable to eat. Dad's news about Curtis has a strangely calming effect on me. He was upset because his mother was in the hospital. An understandable, rational reason for taking a sudden leave that has nothing whatsoever to do with his sexual orientation, a Claymation video, or a student with a crush. Two chapters of history, eight calculus problems,

235

and most of a chem lab write-up later, I come back down for a bowl of cereal. Carrie is on the computer. Mom is on the phone. Dad and the dog are asleep on the couch. As normal as we get. I eat my cereal and walk softly up the stairs. I might actually finish my homework early at this rate. It's sort of sad that I'm excited by that idea.

Private. Personal. None of your goddamned business, but thanks.

The knock on my door comes only moments after I close it, and is immediately followed by my sister entering. Why does she bother to knock?

"We have to talk."

"No, we don't. I have homework I have to do."

"That's school. This is important. You need my help."

"No, Carrie, I need you to go away."

"It took me a long time to figure it all out, but I have it and I want to help. The whole Danielle/Amanda thing. David's letter. I think you just need to be willing to admit that you're gay."

"I'm not gay."

Carrie waves her hand dismissively and sits on my bed. "I've been thinking a lot about this and I want you to know that as your sister I will love you regardless of your sexual orientation. I know you're worried about Mom and Dad, but they'll get it. Dad may take a little time, but Mom will get it right away, and family support is very important for you right now."

"Carrie . . ."

"And I understand that you might not want people at school to know yet . . ."

"Carrie . . ."

She looks up.

"Have you been looking up stuff on the Internet?" I ask her.

"A little."

"You sound like a pamphlet. Web sites about coming out? Gay teens? Suicide rates? That sort of thing?" I know what's out there. I've looked them all up too. She nods. "Why?"

"Because my brother's gay."

Carrie has her serious face on. It is hard to recognize because I haven't seen it often. Most of the time her face is stuck in disdain, occasionally anger, once in a great while actual silliness, but almost never empathetic seriousness.

"Did you read something that was in my desk?"

"Of course I did. You left it sitting in your drawer, what was I supposed to do? It was a love letter, Mitchell. An actual love letter. I almost cried, it was so beautiful. Well, the intention was beautiful, the writing was more like a book report, but it was a love letter. I've never gotten a love letter from anyone. And all this time I was trying to set you up with busty Amanda when you were already seeing someone. How come you didn't trust me enough to tell me?"

"More reasons than I can count, but mostly because I'm not gay. David is—we've worked it out and we're friends, but we're not . . ."

"Lovers?"

"God, no. Nothing has happened. Nothing is going to happen. We are friends. I am straight."

"How are you so sure?"

"I am. I know. Okay?"

"Okay." Carrie looks disappointed. I think she was excited that there might have been something interesting about her brother. A secret life that might have saved me from being the boring dork she orders around.

I should be so pissed at my sister right now. Not only did she go in my desk and read a very private letter, but she's been a total bitch for the last six weeks. I try to summon some anger, but it isn't there. I'm just relieved that someone else knows. I didn't realize until now how badly I've wanted someone else to know. Carrie looks up suddenly. "Can I tell M.C.?"

"Please don't. David hasn't told anyone else. At least I don't think he has."

"But she wouldn't care."

"She might. He's taking her to the prom."

"As friends. There's no romance there at all and she's

fine with it. There's no romance anywhere at the moment. You and David were my best hope."

I don't bring up the possibility of a Danielle romance. "What about Seth?"

"What about him? He's cute and attentive, but he can't complete whole sentences. Unless he gets a brain transplant soon, I'm guessing we've got a week." She smiles. "Maybe six days."

CHAPTER 27

Pure Terror

It was a dark and stormy night

The prom is in six days. Since I have only had a prom date for about a week, I haven't been panicking sufficiently. Then Danielle sent me an e-mail. Now I am sufficiently panicked.

Danielle, who appears to take the prom as seriously as she does her homework, e-mailed me a checklist she found on the Internet. Someone else might be insulted, but I'm surprisingly grateful. It details everything I am supposed to do, from arranging transportation to remembering to ask her the color of her dress so that the corsage will match. It has a timeline that goes from twelve weeks before the prom to the day of (remember to refrigerate corsage, don't forget to tell date that she looks beautiful, don't lock car keys in car). I forward it to David and we spend the afternoon studying this document, particularly the little spreadsheet that outlines projected costs for male and female. Danielle had also sent us a short rant from a prom dress Web site about why boys should pay for most things (mostly because girls have to pay for more expensive haircuts and dresses). Proms appear to exist in some time warp—corsages and girls waiting patiently for their dates to arrive—but even my feminist little sister seems to have bought in and, in truth, I find the haircut explanation compelling given my recent experience.

We are behind. Way behind. But we have a list.

A shot rings out

On Monday night, Danielle calls and says something that chills me to my soul.

"My parents want to meet you."

"Oh."

"Tomorrow. For dinner."

"Really? Why?"

"Maybe because you are taking me to the prom on Saturday. You know my dad's a minister, right? He's also a prick. Don't listen to a thing he says. He's used to making pronouncements from his pulpit and he believes that everyone cares what he thinks."

I sort of met Danielle's mom last week when we were studying buttons at her house, but it was just a quick "Hi Mom, this is Mitchell" and her dad wasn't home.

Tomorrow is also the day when I have to go sit in Sorrelson's office with the Judicial Board. Maybe I'll get lucky and a meteorite will crash into the planet and destroy all life as we know it.

A blood-curdling scream echoes in the empty house

11:20. Tuesday. I am standing in front of Sorrelson's office. The door is closed. The seven members of the Judicial Board are crammed inside the tiny room being briefed on the facts of the case. I've watched them all arrive, one by one. The two seniors are quiet, earnest types who were elected because of their unwavering lack of humor. The other junior is Hannah, who Carrie insists is a lesbian and militant feminist but who looks awfully normal to me. The lone sophomore is a girl named Sophie, who looks embarrassed about the whole thing. Sorrelson and Coach Hayes are the designated adults. Louis is late and the last to get there.

The door swings open. In a small miracle of engineering, eight chairs have been shoehorned into Sorrelson's office. Sorrelson sits at his desk between the two uncomfortable-looking seniors. The coach and Louis are at the far wall. Both of the girls are sitting opposite the desk cross-legged because there isn't enough room for their feet. I squeeze past the chair at the door. Sorrelson motions for me to close the door behind me, and I reach back and pull it shut. It makes a loud and ominous thud. I sit in the chair, one leg touching the nearest senior, the other pinned by the corner of the desk. The smell in the room is already oppressive.

"I have explained the situation to the board. They would like to ask a few questions."

"Did they watch the film?"

"Louis has, of course, because he was in class. No one else. I didn't feel it was necessary. I told them what was relevant about it."

"Isn't it hard to talk about whether it is offensive if no one has seen it?" I don't mean for the question to sound rude, but it seems so obvious that I can't help but ask.

"It is offensive," Sorrelson insists. "People were offended."

"I think the question," one of the seniors begins, "is whether the movie was intended to be offensive."

"I think that's irrelevant," says Sorrelson.

The senior goes back to staring at the floor.

"Mitchell, would you like to explain why you decided to turn in a Claymation project rather than a paper?" The coach is smiling encouragingly.

I try to remember. Saying that I did it so I wouldn't have to read the book doesn't sound like a good answer.

"I was trying to do something a little different."

"Well, you did that," Sorrelson interrupts. I'm beginning to sense how these meetings go.

"I don't even know why we are here," Hannah says, clearly frustrated and utterly unintimidated. "If you want to punish the guy for making a funny film, just do it, and stop pretending you care what we think."

"That's not fair. We do care what you think. You are

elected members of the Judicial Board of this school and you have the responsibility to protect the integrity of the values this school holds dear . . ." Sorrelson is angry and spitting again.

"Look," says the other senior, who seems to have grown a backbone in the last few minutes, "I don't care what the stupid clay figures were doing. It was an English assignment and his teacher thought it was fine and no one lost a limb or anything, so everybody should just calm down and let us go to lunch."

"This is important, Jordon. Lunch can wait," scolds the first senior.

"It's a formality to give the administration a cover of student participation. They don't care what we think," Hannah fumes.

"All I'm saying," the first senior says, "is that this case has no merit. It's an academic issue, not a Judicial Board thing. Mitchell didn't break any rules."

Sorrelson, sensing he is losing control of the meeting, tries to fix the senior with his angry eye. "In our handbook it clearly states that we respect all religious views. Tolerance is a key value of our community."

"What about tolerance of Mitchell's ideas? His creative expression?" the senior counters.

"Blasphemy is not tolerable."

Hannah sighs loudly enough to halt the argument. "This is so stupid. We don't even know what was in the film."

"I just want to say that I agree with everything every-one has said so far," the sophomore adds.

Louis rolls his eyes, sits up straight, and turns toward the desk. "Mr. Sorrelson, sir. I appreciate the role of values in education. I appreciate what an important role the Judicial Board plays in the life of this school. I, for one, am proud to sit on it . . ."

"And to have appeared before it six times in the last three years," interjects Coach Hayes, still smiling.

"But let's be honest, sir," Louis continues, ignoring the interruption. "This is not about religious tolerance. It is not about creative expression. You are once again sacrific-ing the good of a student on the altar of fund-raising. Some wealthy donors get a bug up their butt because they heard a rumor that a student project dared to include *SATAN*—ooh, and they call you up and off you go tying poor little Mitchell Wells to the stake to protect your large bottom line."

"It's always about the complaining parent; why aren't you protecting your students?" Hannah asks in a voice that is almost a scream. She and Louis are on a roll. Revolution is in the air.

"Look at this young man. This boy. This student." Louis gestures toward me across the office. "How can you sacrifice poor little Mitchell Wells for a few more bucks in the annual fund? Yes, he's a virgin, but we don't sacrifice virgins anymore. And now he's dating an actual female, not even a bad-looking one, and yes, we are stunned and wonder what she sees in this skinny blaspheming pornographer who hasn't had a date in his skinny little life, but now he has a chance and you, Mr. Sorrelson, are going to ruin that for him. Where is your compassion?"

"Free Mitchell Wells!" screams Hannah, banging her fist on the desk.

"I think we are about done here," Sorrelson says, glaring at Hannah, then Louis. "Mr. Wells, this board will make its recommendation to Dr. VandeNeer within the week. Then it will be up to the headmaster, I mean our CEO, to decide what disciplinary actions should be taken."

"Told you we were wasting our time," Hannah growls once more as she stands on her chair to climb out of the office.

"I think that went well," Louis tells me as we walk to lunch. "Sometimes we get into really nasty arguments."

Inquisition to inquisition

I am once again carless, since Carrie has a minimum of seven things planned for this evening and there is no way she can get a ride to any of them, but Danielle's suggestion that I just ride home with her after school prevents what would otherwise be a justifiable case of sororicide. David's car passes us on our way up to the parking lot. Carrie and M.C. are both riding in the backseat and my place is empty. None of them look our way and I pretend I don't notice.

Danielle's mother meets us at the door. She is gorgeous. Stop-and-stare-on-the-street gorgeous. There is no way she is my mom's age. She must have had Danielle when she was six. I've never had a thing about anyone's mother. Older is just old. But Danielle's mother—"Call me Paige," she insists—makes me unbearably uncomfortable. She is casual elegance in gray pants and a white blouse cut low enough to show much more cleavage than I'm used to seeing. I've never complained about revealing clothing, I'm seventeen, but sometimes even I could admit that too much boob display looks cheap and tacky. Not *this* boob display. Maybe it's the shirt. *Expensive* boob display. Her face is wrinkle-free and she isn't wearing makeup. She looks healthy and confident, and if I'm thinking my girlfriend's mother is sexy, is there something wrong with me?

"Hi. I'm Mitchell," I say.

"I know," she says, laughing. "Come in. Reverend Walker will be home in just a few minutes. Would you like something to drink?"

Can I ask for hard alcohol? I think I might need it.

I glance over at Danielle, who, to my relief, looks very much like a seventeen-year-old girl. A seventeen-year-old girl, in this case, who is really annoyed and embarrassed by her parents. She grabs my hand and drags me downstairs to the living room. "We're downstairs," she calls to her mother, as if she couldn't see that. At the bottom of the stairs, out of sight, she kisses me.

"We're studying," she yells back upstairs. That might be more convincing if we hadn't left our backpacks upstairs in the hallway.

◉   ◉   ◉

It's more like an hour and a half before the reverend comes home and we are called upstairs for dinner. There is something a little tense about talking to someone's parents right after you've been mauling their daughter on the downstairs couch. Do they know? Do they suspect? The reverend is a little chubby around the middle but he carries it with authority and moves with a smooth motion that is almost graceful. He has thinning white hair that he wears closely cropped, and his large smile seems genuine.

The table is set. There are wineglasses, cloth napkins, china. "We eat like this every night," Danielle says, sighing. "My parents think dinner is always a big deal."

Dinner is delicious. It's just a roast chicken, potatoes, and vegetables, but they are cooked perfectly, the meat juicy, the vegetables steamed but not mushy. At first I'm afraid to help myself because the food is so beautifully displayed on the serving platters, but everyone is dishing it out onto plates like it's no big deal. If this is normal for the Walkers, I will never be able to invite Danielle to eat at my house.

I so don't want to like these two adults. Danielle certainly doesn't appear to. She answers their questions sullenly, but they keep up a light banter despite her. Reverend Walker is a natural storyteller, spinning out small anecdotes into very funny, long stories. There's cake for dessert. Everyone helps clear the table. It is all going so well. Then the reverend corners me in the kitchen.

"You know, Mitch," he says confidentially, "I run a large church. Lots of opinions, all kinds of people. Now, I don't know you yet, Mitch, but you seem like a polite young man. If Danielle wants you to take her to this dance, I've got no problem. But we keep a tight leash on our little girl. She doesn't like it, but it's who we are. We call that good parenting.

"Now, Danielle's a little mad at me because her mother and I felt the need to let the school know what we thought about your film project. It was nothing personal, you realize, but we feel a responsibility to speak for our faith community. Young people, they think everything's okay. They don't always understand the big picture, the perspective, that those of us with less hair can sometimes see. There are rules—rules right there in the book, and we just can't say, 'Nah, don't want to bother with them.' It's all or nuthin' and I'm still an 'all' person. You take all this talk about homosexuals." He breaks the word into pieces—*ho-mo-sex-shuls*—and I can hear his preaching voice rising. "I've got nothing against them. We love our neighbors and if our daughter turned out to be a lez-bee-ann, would I still love her? Of course I would. But here's the bigger picture. It's not about love, it's about pro-mo-scew-a-tee. About values. About fam-ee-lee."

"Dad, would you please leave Mitchell alone?"

"We're just talking, honey."

"It's a school night. We have homework to do."

For the first time in my life, I can't wait to write my English paper.

CHAPTER 28

WQQD

A short ugly scene late at night in my driveway

It is near midnight when Danielle drives me home. We don't talk much. Given how she drives, I am careful not to distract her. Instead I watch her face as it's illuminated by the streetlights we pass, which create a slow strobe-like effect. I can't tell whether she can feel me looking at her. As she pulls into the driveway, the headlights settle on a person standing where there shouldn't be anyone. David is standing in my driveway. There are at least three things wrong with this picture:

1) It is close to midnight. No one, not even me, knew I would be out this late. How long has he been standing in my driveway? Has he been standing the whole time?

2) David knew I was with Danielle. He knew I didn't have a car. If nothing else, he could have

counted. Two cars, I'm not home, I didn't drive.

Was he waiting for both of us?

3) Where is David's car?

All of this passes through my brain as I sit next to Danielle, staring at the person who is supposed to be my best friend. Danielle looks at me for an answer, but I don't know how to respond. Finally, I get out of the car, but Danielle doesn't follow me. She also doesn't turn off the engine.

"Hi," is all I can think to say.

"Good morning," David answers. He is not slurring his words, but he's definitely drunk.

"What's going on?"

"Oh, not much. How was your date?"

"We were studying."

"Uh-huh. Learn much?"

"Are you trying to be a jerk?"

David steadies himself and looks at me, but I can't make out his expression. The mixture of darkness and bright headlights makes his glasses glow, but the lower half of his face is a shadow.

"I came to see how your English paper's coming. I didn't want you to forget about it."

"You show up drunk in my driveway at midnight to save my English grade?"

"I felt responsible."

"Where is your car?"

David points somewhere to his left. "That way. I didn't want Ty and Liz to wake up." This is new. I don't think David has ever referred to my parents by their first names. He leans toward me and whispers, "Ty thinks I'm gay."

"You *are* gay."

"Shhh." He motions toward the car. "Has she told everybody yet?"

"I haven't told her."

"Truth?"

"Truth."

"Why not?"

"You told me not to."

"Why do you do everything I tell you to do?"

Neither of us has moved since we got out of the car. We are standing a good six feet away from each other. The space between us is a wall of light. If you had asked me yesterday, I would have told you that I know everything about David Bryant, that there was nothing he could do that would surprise me. But I don't know this guy in my driveway. He doesn't even look familiar, standing in his logoless sweatshirt, calm and angry. I wonder how much of our conversation Danielle can hear. What do we look like posed this way, framed by the headlights of her car?

"What were you listening to in the car?"

"Who cares? The radio."

"WQQD, right?"

"Probably."

"It sucks."

"We could change the station."

"No," David shouts. "We can't. We all have to listen to it. That's the point. I have to listen to sucky music, you have to stick your tongue in Danielle's mouth, we have to make at least an A– in English or we will never get into law school . . ." David stops suddenly and his expression changes. "Excuse me," he says a little less loudly, "I have to puke."

Only David would start the sentence I have to puke with an "excuse me."

I cross the path of the headlights and try to guide him over to what's left of the shrubs I ran over last fall.

"No—not in that bush," he says, sounding very concerned. "I've already puked there." He points across the driveway. "This one over here needs some too."

I help him across the driveway and wait quietly beside him as he retches into the matching shrub remnant. After a few minutes he stands up, looking a little less angry.

"I'll go home," he says softly.

"You are not driving home."

"I'm not sleeping here."

"Danielle and I will drive you."

"I can drive. I'm not that bad."

"I will tackle you and take away your car keys. You are not driving."

There is a long pause. His face is a complete blank. "I suck."

"You're just drunk."

"No, I'm a shit. A total shit. I'm supposed to be your friend."

"You *are* my friend."

"I am?"

"Yes, you're my best friend."

"Still?"

"Yes. David, I still need you to be my friend. Did you just puke on my shoe?"

"A little."

I think his sudden turn to the maudlin is worse than his anger. I wipe my shoe off on the grass, put a hand on David's arm, and lead him over to Danielle's car. Danielle's door opens—she must have been watching all of this. She isn't smiling, but she doesn't seem angry. She gets out and opens the door for David and I guide him into the backseat. He's still mumbling about what a shitty friend he is and how I should punch him or something, but he stays upright. I don't bother with the seat belt. For a moment I wonder if I should ride in the back with him, but I don't. Danielle doesn't ask the plan, and I don't even ask whether she minds driving David home and then dropping me back here again. I could have put him in my car, but I didn't think of that until now. The truth is I don't want to take him by myself. Maybe Danielle senses this.

Nobody talks on the way to David's house. When we get there, he climbs out of the car and walks to his door. I swallow hard, trying not to imagine what it feels like to have to make that walk with Danielle and me watching him. He never turns around. We are too far away to hear the slam of the door, but part of me feels it.

Danielle doesn't ask any questions on the way home. We talk in near whispers about the most normal things we can come up with—school and homework and whether I've rented my tux. "It's late," she says, leaning over and kissing me softly.

"Thank you," I say. I don't watch her car pull away.

CHAPTER 29

Prom and Punishment

A disaster in three acts, two of which take place in the bathroom at the Sheraton Hotel, which isn't bad as bathrooms go, but not where I was hoping to spend my prom

Act 1: I pee on my pants

Okay, so I peed on my pants.

I am standing in the bathroom at my junior prom, the prom that is supposed to be one of the high points of my high-school career, the prom that has cost me the entirety of my savings, the prom to which I have brought the very person I have dreamed about dating since fifth grade, the prom that has now surpassed my fourth-grade birthday party as the single worst event of my life. I am standing in the bathroom at my junior prom and I have peed on my pants.

Short of shitting my pants, this is about as bad as it gets.

I am wearing white pants.

I wanted to get a black tuxedo. A traditional, just like everyone else, black tuxedo. However, by the time David and I finally got ourselves to Formal Deluxe, there was nothing in my size except white or lime green, and I was not up to looking like a lounge act. So I did the sensible thing. I panicked and called my mother. Within ten minutes, my mother, my sister, and our dog were standing in the lobby of Formal Deluxe discussing the options with a much too serious Mr. Killhorne, who kept insisting that we call him Jake.

My mother argued that I could just wear my good suit, which was admittedly a little small on me and made of a very nice polyester blend but would be much cheaper. She was sure that other people would be in suits, since that was something that happened a lot when she went to proms in the early part of the Pleistocene.

Carrie, being the kind of sixteen-year-old girl who knows enough to ignore her mother entirely, suggested the lime green on the grounds that if you are going to look geeky, you should look like you are trying to look geeky and not like you geeked by accident.

Both David and the dog stood there looking embarrassed and somewhat bored. Neither seemed convinced about the gravity of this crisis.

Jake told us that the white tux looks distinguished and insisted that he had rented a lot of them already for this very prom.

I went for the white tux. It was, as Jake pointed out, only a little more expensive.

I am, of course, the only one at the prom wearing white. There are a number of people who chose interesting pastel shades. Lime green would have fit right in.

If not for its exceptional ability to display pee stains, the whiteness of my tux would have been but a small footnote to the evening, which actually started out all right.

David and I hadn't talked much about what had happened in my driveway. Mostly we just pretended it hadn't happened. But when he showed up at my house on prom night to pry me loose from my bedroom, where I had retreated in total panic, I was genuinely relieved to see him. My mother declared us adorable in our tuxes and insisted on taking pictures of us. Adorable was not the effect either of us was looking for. It was a little strange to pose for pictures with David without our dates. In them we are standing side by side, trying hard to look like we aren't taking each other to the prom. Then we drove to M.C.'s house and her father took pictures of the three of us, which was equally awkward since, at least in theory, M.C. was David's date. By the time we made it to Danielle's house for more pictures, we were thirty minutes late for dinner. These few hours are the best documented of my life.

After much discussion and a careful review of our present financial situation, David and I had geeked and decided not to rent a limo. Instead David borrowed his father's car, a Honda Civic. Nevertheless, I felt pretty grown-up climbing out of the car and holding the door for my date as we walked into Georgio's. At least we weren't forced to take the minivan. I don't remember much from dinner except that I drank a lot of water and nobody spoke much. And it was expensive. Really expensive. We knew it would be and we brought enough money, but I wasn't prepared for how large that stack of tens and twenties would look when we had to lay it down on the table. I'm pretty sure we ate something.

I look down at my pants leg. I convince myself that no one will notice. It's a dark room. If someone asks, I'll say that I spilled water on myself while washing my hands. The faucet spurted out suddenly. Or maybe I spilled a drink on my pants and was trying to wash out the stain. They are rented pants; it would make sense that I would worry about staining. I sit in the stall and practice. "God, can you believe it? Spilled the drink right on my pants. How embarrassing can you get, right down the leg. Looks like I pissed on myself." I would use the word "pissed," get in what it looks like first. Good strategy.

At least I didn't pee on myself at the urinals. I don't use urinals. I haven't since I was about eight. They are way too public. I always choose a stall and, once safely inside, I undo my pants and let them fall down to about the level of my knees. This way they are out of the way, beneath the level of the seat. Then all I have to do is make sure I aim for the water. This method has worked for years. No mishaps. But somehow tonight I wasn't looking, and I peed directly into the folds of my open pants, which were arranged just perfectly like a large open flower to catch my pee. By the time I noticed, a large pool had collected in one leg along the top edge, and it was streaming down over my shoe and onto the floor. This was not an oops-I-got-a-few-drops-on-myself moment. I have emptied my entire bladder onto my pants.

I look down at my still-wet leg again, hoping it has already, out of sympathy, defied the laws of physics and dried. I can't believe how thoroughly I have soaked my pants. I know I drank a lot of water at dinner, but it looks as if I dumped all of it on myself. It isn't just the amount of water I drank that has driven me to the bathroom.

◉ ◎ ◉

In order to get into the prom, we have to pass through an elaborate security checkpoint manned by teachers in suits and dresses who clearly aren't being paid enough for this duty. Ms. Bexter is there, looking a little lost without a chalkboard behind her, next to Ms. Kalikowski, who at least tries to smile. We are sniffed for alcohol, purses are screened for contraband, and our prom tickets are scrutinized carefully, as if there were a large black-market operation for forging passes. Since the teachers already know us well enough to realize that we are way too docile to show up drunk for the prom, we get waved through with a minimal amount of fuss but enough so we won't feel insulted. My guess is that they frisked Louis when he arrived. Danielle and M.C. disappear into the bathroom as soon as we walk through the door. I look at David.

"Are we having fun?" I ask.

"Did you expect to?" he replies.

"I guess so. Aren't we supposed to?"

David takes off his glasses and polishes them on his cummerbund. "No. No one actually likes their prom. It's not meant to be fun. It's meant to be a ritual, like slaughtering hecatombs of cattle to the gods in the *Iliad*. We're here because we feel that we are supposed to be here and that's all. It's why we all wear the same stupid clothes, listen to the same grating music, and watch the same lame television shows. We"—he pauses for dramatic effect—"are teenagers. Hallelujah and praise the Lord."

Danielle emerges from the bathroom with M.C. in tow. Danielle. Maybe *I'm* here to be with Danielle. At that moment, Ryan walks in with his date. She's tall, blond, thin—basically a supermodel. I'm not the only one who stares. Danielle grabs M.C.'s hand and heads back to the bathroom.

"Danielle and M.C. seem to be getting along pretty well," observes David. He is unusually talkative this evening.

We take a swing past the snack table and pick up soda and hors d'oeuvres, noting that the plastic cups and paper napkins are of exceptionally high quality—for plastic cups and paper napkins. The napkins have the date and theme stamped on them. Knowing that Danielle was responsible for the theme, we take a moment to appreciate the decor: little fake bridges, travel posters of St. Mark's Square, and a full-size gondola where each happy couple will sit for the oh-so-romantic picture to commemorate the event. Clearly not Paris. We find a small table off to one side, place our finger foods on the mauve tablecloth, and wait for the women to return.

"This could be a long night," I tell David.

"They are all the same length," he replies factually. "An hour is an hour is an hour."

◉ ◎ ◉

M.C. comes back from the bathroom alone.

"Danielle says she'll be out in a minute," she tells us. "In old movies girls are always saying they have to powder their noses. Is there a historical reason that we don't powder noses anymore, or do we just have shinier noses in this century?"

"It was just a euphemism for pissing," David says distractedly.

"Danielle's pissing. Doesn't sound as polite. Besides, she's not. She's talking to Nicole." M.C. sits between David and me.

"Should we dance?" David asks.

"Ménage a trois?" M.C. suggests.

I tell M.C. thanks, but I'll wait for Danielle to finish powdering her nose or pissing or whatever she's doing. I watch David and M.C. dance. David's a little stiff but he doesn't look self-conscious. M.C. actually has a sense of rhythm. Even with her hair styled, her face made-up, and the tiny straps of her prom dress across her bare shoulders, she is still amazingly M.C., smiling and swirling and swaying her shoulders the way she would in our living room or in the hallway at school or anywhere the mood strikes her. Here, with an actual band and a dance floor full of dressed-up people, it's as if everyone else finally hears the music she has been hearing in her head.

A second couple moves onto the dance floor, blocking my view of M.C. A very tall Peter clutches a diminutive, barely dressed Amanda and neither of them looks my way. Amanda appears enraptured; her eyes rarely leave Peter's face. Peter is all smirks. They are dancing, but not moving much, which might be appropriate if it were a slow song. The more interesting dance is between Amanda and her dress—they often seem to be moving in opposite directions. Amanda leans, and the slit on the side swirls open around a bare thigh. The halter, which was never designed for the load it's carrying, hangs on valiantly as Amanda stands on her toes to kiss Peter. Peter turns her slightly and I am facing the line of her bare spine, topped by her brown hair and then diving dramatically, only meeting cloth at the last possible moment before revealing the full rise of her butt cheeks, neatly outlined by the tight material stretched mercilessly across them.

A hand on my shoulder. Danielle has returned from the ladies' room. She does not look happy. I ask her to dance. "Maybe in a few minutes," she says. She doesn't look at me; she stares at the floor, the band, the wall beyond me, anywhere but my eyes. I've never wanted to touch someone so badly in my life. I know that all the turmoil I see in her face has nothing to do with me, but I still want to hold her and tell her it will all be okay. She looks torn apart. All I feel is empty.

◉ ◉ ◉

So this is my prom. I sit with David as the entire school watches the Danielle and Ryan show. There's a brief confrontation between the two in the hallway, followed by Danielle sobbing in the bathroom and Ryan pacing angrily. There are a few minutes of tense quiet as Danielle returns to sit with me at the table and pretends that I really am her date. An unusual amount of time is spent by both parties in their respective bathrooms. Nicole is resurrected from her role as bitch traitor and becomes the chief go-between for both sides. The goings-on might be fascinating for a disinterested third party to observe, but despite my third-party status, I'm not exactly disinterested. And I already know what all this means: my time is up.

Scurrying from Danielle's semi-permanent camp in the ladies' room to Ryan's table, which is mostly populated by guys whose dates are elsewhere, Nicole, teenage diplo-mat, negotiates. Within an hour she has brokered the deal. When she comes to tell me the verdict, how true love has once again gained ascendance, she looks at me with gen-uine pity. She doesn't actually tell me that I'm dumped; we have to speak in code. Danielle has a headache and needs to leave. Of course I understand. I volunteer to drive her home, seeing that I was her nominal date, but Nicole dis-misses that option quickly. I decide not to argue. I wonder what they did with Ryan's date.

"Do you want to just go home?" David asks.

"No, I'll just sit here. It can't get worse."

M.C. looks like she's about to cry, purely from sympathy. David, sensing that maybe I need a moment, escorts her to the dance floor and dutifully slow-dances with her. I watch them, wondering why I haven't burst out in tears yet.

I then do what all sensible people do when they are dumped at their prom. I go to the bathroom and pee on my own pants, just to prove that it can, in fact, get worse.

Act 2: It gets worse

David eventually comes to find me.

"Are you okay?"

No. I'm clearly not okay. I've been dumped, I peed on myself, and my pants leg, which is finally drying, is devel-oping a very noticeable yellow stain.

"Mitchell, are you having diarrhea or something?"

"No, I'm fine," I tell him. It is not a convincing statement. We stand there for a while on either side of the stall door.

"Come on, Mitchell. You have to come out of there."

"I can't."

"Why not?"

"I've, um, spilled something on my pants."

Mercifully, David doesn't ask me what I spilled. He gets a paper towel, runs it under the water for a second, and lobs it over the door to me. I do my best to rub the yellowing stain, but now it just looks wet again.

I come out of the stall. David looks at me for a full ten seconds before he has any visible reaction. "Christ. Maybe I should drive home and get you new pants."

I go back into the stall.

Two guys come in, use the urinals, and leave without washing their hands. Usually it is the kind of thing that David would comment on.

"Look," David starts, "we'll just walk straight out to the car. No one will notice."

"Has Danielle left?"

"Who the hell cares?"

"I do."

"You shouldn't. She was using you to get back at Ryan. Everybody knew it."

"I didn't."

"You should have."

"I liked her." I nearly choke on the past tense.

"She's shallow, manipulative, and self-centered. You liked her because she's popular and because she let you touch her tits."

I've never seen David this angry. Actually, I'm not really seeing him at all because we're on opposite sides of the stall door, but this is a new tone of voice for him. All I can manage is another squeaky, "I liked her."

"Whatever. Let's just go home."

"I can't."

"Jesus, Mitchell. Look, it's embarrassing, it's mean, she's a bitch, get over it. It isn't like you were married or anything."

"What's with you? I just broke up with someone I really liked."

"Well, technically, she broke up with you."

"Thanks. Like I wasn't clear. You just don't get it because you haven't been there. You don't know what it's like to get your heart stomped on."

David is silent, and I wish I could see his face. When he finally speaks, he's back to monotone, as if he has stripped all emotion from the words. "First of all, 'stomping on hearts' is about the lamest cliché I've ever heard. Second of all, I know a lot about having my heart stomped on and you, of all people, know that. Third of all, you fucking pissed on your pants." With that, he walks out of the bathroom.

I sit in the stall. This time I cry.

Act 3: Why Louis is a prick

It's hard to give yourself much credit for simply opening a door, but deciding to leave the bathroom may be the single bravest thing I will ever do in my life. When the tears finally stop, I sit for a moment and try to collect myself. I practice my breathing while I wait through a few more urinations and one person vomiting into the sink. When everyone is gone, I finally slink out of the stall and make one more attempt to wash off my pants. They don't smell too bad and they aren't soaking, but there's still a large discoloration stretching from my crotch to my ankle. I try standing under the hand dryer, but it's too far up the wall to do much good. It still looks like I peed on my pants. But it doesn't matter. I have to find David. I'm not sure what I'll say to him when I find him, but I have to find him. I have to find David. I use this as a mantra, to keep me focused. I have to find David. I have to find David.

"Take a deep breath and open the door," I tell myself. I repeat these instructions in a whisper three times. Finally, I take one deep breath and open the door.

Louis is, of course, standing on the other side of the door.

His eyes are drawn immediately to the wet spot on my pants leg. Immediately. No passing go, no 200 bucks. "You pissed on yourself."

"I was washing my hands . . . I spilled my drink and . . ."

"Bullshit, you pissed on yourself." It is as definitive an accusation as you can get. I wither.

269

"Could you be a bigger loser?" The answer appears to be no. Louis shakes his head and I stare at the floor in an effort to keep myself from breaking into tears again.

"Stay here," he commands. "No, actually, go sit in the stall for a minute, I'll be right back."

I know that Louis is the person I trust least in the whole world. I know that he has never done or said anything to me that anyone would consider nice. Nevertheless, I go sit in the stall and wait for him.

He returns carrying a large plastic cup.

"Get your butt out here," he growls and I obey. "We have to get you out of here. Here's how we're going to do it. This is seltzer; it won't stain." He pauses as Michael Joseph walks into the bathroom. "Yo, Joseph Michael, don't piss yourself," Louis calls out. Michael responds with his middle finger.

Louis continues in a whisper. "As we walk out, call me a faggot. Don't worry about what happens next. In three minutes, we'll be out on the sidewalk, no one will know. Ready?"

Well, no. I don't want to call Louis a faggot. It's not a word I can use anymore.

"Louis." That's my voice. I wasn't expecting it.

"Don't thank me. I can't stand that mushy stuff."

"I don't want to call you a faggot."

He looks at me as if he is about to say something, but he doesn't. He scratches the thin goatee that adorns his chubby chin. " 'Asshole' will do."

"How about 'prick'?"

"Even better." An actual non-malicious smile.

We walk out the door. "You prick," I say as loudly as I can. It isn't really loud, but it's audible.

Louis turns, throws the water at me, places his face less than three inches from mine and growls, "Did you call me a prick?"

The water hits me square in the chest, but no one had been watching closely enough to notice that I had come out of the bathroom with a wet leg. I have cover.

Louis repeats his growl louder. "Did you call me a prick?"

I don't have to respond. Suddenly five or six guys are dragging Louis away. Several of them try to hold me back as well, but since I haven't made any motion toward Louis, they don't have much to do.

It takes Mr. Sorrelson, the designated prom heavy, a few minutes to realize that something is going on and make his way over to us.

"Mr. Wells, what happened?" he barks.

Nothing comes to me, so I say, "Nothing."

"You're wet."

"Someone spilled a drink on me." I'm beginning to shake. I'm hoping that it isn't visible. Louis has disappeared.

"We don't tolerate fighting."

"I wasn't fighting."

The small crowd that had gathered a moment ago has conveniently dispersed. No available witnesses. I'm the only one who seems to have been caught. Sorrelson looks around. He sniffs as if it might trigger some deeply buried bloodhound instinct. He seems to be at a loss for what to do. He didn't see Louis, so he doesn't have a conflict to settle here. All he has is me, standing there shaking, dripping seltzer from my white tuxedo.

"Maybe you should call it a night, Mr. Wells. I may need to speak to you again on Monday, so don't think this little incident is over."

Even I can tell this little incident is over. At this point, it hardly matters—how much more trouble can I be in? This would just be a small footnote to my file. I follow Sorrelson to the door, looking as if I'm upset to leave.

He stops suddenly. "Where's your date?"

I shrug. He raises one eyebrow, but doesn't respond.

"Let me tell my ride I'm leaving." He watches me closely from his post near the door, in case I make a break for the dance floor or something. I find M.C. at our table, but no David.

"He took off. A few minutes ago." She looks more bewildered than upset.

"He just left us here?"

"Maybe it was something I said."

I swallow hard. "It wasn't something you said. Look, I'm being kicked out. Don't laugh. It's a long story. Is there someone who can give you a ride home? I need to find David."

"I'll come with you." M.C. reaches up and takes my hand. Her fingers slide in between mine easily, comfortably, as if they did this all the time.

"I'll have Sorrelson call us a cab," I tell her, and we both smile. Not quite a laugh, but a real, unforced smile. The first one I remember all day.

CHAPTER 30

Monosyllabic Utterances

Guys

Maybe David and I are guys after all. We self-parked. It wasn't humiliating enough for us to arrive in a Honda; we had to skip the valet too. Climbing out of the Civic in prom gowns would have been less than glamorous, but at least we could have walked into the elegant lobby, down the plush maroon carpet, and made a proper entrance. Instead, David pulled into the parking deck and our dates had to walk, in high heels, up two flights of dingy, poorly lit stairs that smelled like someone had been sick in them recently, before finally arriving through a side door next to the bathrooms.

"He had to have taken the car." M.C. looks cold in the air-conditioned lobby, so I slip off my jacket and place it around her shoulders. Maybe I should have asked first. She seems surprised by my chivalry, but not upset, and she slides her arms into the sleeves. The jacket may fit her better than me. She definitely looks cuter in it.

"Maybe he's sitting in the car waiting for us."

We agree that I at least have to check. I leave M.C. standing in the lobby, in case he comes back. The stairs seem even darker now and the smell is more complex— still vomit, but now with undertones of pot.

The car isn't there.

I stand in the space where it should have been. I recheck the signs to make sure I'm on the right level. I'm in the right place. The car is just gone. I didn't expect it to be here, but somehow I'm more disturbed by the reality of the empty parking space than I was by the thought of it. David took the car and left me here. He must have been really pissed off. I know what David eats for lunch, I know what he means when he shrugs, I know his batting average, and which episode of *Pib and Pog* is his favorite, but I have no idea what he's thinking right now. I'm not sure I know anything about my best friend.

Sex

I hear the beep of a car alarm being deactivated, followed by the click of a door being unlocked. Door slams, engine revs. Normal on the surface feels portentous here in the depths of the parking deck.

With a squeal of tires, a familiar Porsche pulls up next to me.

"Lost something?" Best friend, girlfriend, car. I nod. Nicole's hair has lost some of the composure it had earlier in the evening, as if someone has been pawing it. There's some story here—some sequence of events that led her to get her own car from the garage and leave by herself—but not one that I can guess from looking at her face. She seems only half-interested in whether I answer her question. She knows at least part of why I'm standing here by myself.

"Carson's. After-party. Ditch this lame-ass event. Hop in." Nicole's not one for full sentences.

For a moment I imagine myself a different Mitchell, one who would "hop in" to Nicole's Porsche on my way to an after-party that the real Mitchell never would be invited to, watching her long tan legs work the gears. She looks like money, even without the Porsche as backdrop. Her skin is smooth and unblemished, her clothes are expensive and fit her perfectly, but worn with the casualness of not having to worry about such things. My fantasy has worked itself all the way up to the after question about whether this was just mercy sex when she interrupts.

"Mitch?"

I'd like to be a different Mitchell, but I'm not Mitch. I say, "Thanks, but . . ." and can't seem to finish the sentence. She doesn't seem fazed.

"Catch you later," she says, but she doesn't mean it. I don't expect her to ever speak to me again. She was just offering a ride to a schlep her friend dumped.

"Gotta go. Party goin' on." She pulls away. I head back up the stairs.

No

When I reenter the lobby, M.C. isn't alone, but David isn't back. The blond male standing beside her is Louis. I almost don't recognize him because he is standing still, not gesturing, not talking.

"You're still here," he states quietly, like he didn't think I should be.

"I'm leaving. We were just trying to find David."

"I was just asking M.C. if she would like to stay."

"I think your date might mind," M.C. says in a very flat tone.

"She would," he answers, looking M.C. straight in the face.

"I'm going with Mitchell." M.C.'s voice is firm, leaving no room for even Louis to argue. "We're going to see if we can find David."

"Okay," Louis says with a forced casualness. "I'll see you Monday."

Nobody moves.

Finally, M.C. takes my hand again. "Bye," she says, and walks us out of the lobby. Neither of us looks back.

Friend

M.C. shrugs. It's a David sort of shrug. I don't ask her about what was happening with Louis back there.

"Did you try calling him?" she asks.

"He doesn't carry a cell."

"Really?"

"Really."

"We could call my parents. Or yours," M.C. suggests.

"I need to find David."

"We could walk. David doesn't live that far from here." M.C. is being unusually reasonable.

"Why didn't he walk, then?"

"I think he may have been upset. You look pretty upset too. Would you please stop pacing? If that were forward motion, we could be there already."

I think she means this as a joke. I look up and she is smiling, but I'm not going to relax that easily.

"Come on, the walk will do you good. Dry you off and everything."

I shove my hands in my pockets and walk beside M.C. We must look odd walking down the street, tux and prom gown. If I wasn't feeling like such a shit, I might be able to see some humor in all of this. I try to sort out the noises in my head. What did I say to David? Had I really stomped on his heart? Did I really use the phrase "stomped on my heart"? Am I really a heart stomper? How did I pee on my own pants? I look at M.C., who still seems lost in her own thoughts. She must realize I'm looking at her, because she changes into her smile.

"How are you holding up?" she asks.

"Oh, I'm fine. I'm dropping out of school as of Monday, and I'm never leaving my room again, but I have a pretty nice room and I'm sure my parents won't mind me staying there forever."

"It's not that bad."

"Oh, come on. It's pretty bad."

M.C. nods. "Yeah, it's bad. But at least it wasn't you—I mean, people have to blame Danielle for being cruel enough to dump you at the prom."

"I guess this hasn't exactly been the prom of your dreams either?"

M.C. smiles again. "I'm not sure what I expected, but this is a little different than I imagined. I feel a little badly about Louis. He looked really sad when I left with you."

"He told me that you were the one he wanted to take to the prom."

"I know. That's because of the ski trip thing."

"The guy from the ski trip. That was Louis?"

"You didn't know? He didn't tell you?"

"No."

"You're going to think I'm horrible."

"Mostly I'm just freaked out that you were willing to kiss Louis."

"Oh, come on. Like you haven't been sharing saliva with Danielle for two weeks."

"One of those choices seems more hygienic."

"Whatever. It was all so stupid. We were on this ski trip. And I guess I was flirting with this guy—the guy we saw when we went to get ice cream. Do you remember? But he was only interested in Carrie, and when he saw that was no go, he stopped even pretending to talk to me. I was feeling about *this* high, because no one is ever interested in me.

I'm always the tag-along. Carrie's friend. And I end up sitting there and talking to Louis, who was sort of listening, and then he leans over and kisses me, and I liked the attention but not particularly Louis, and maybe that makes me the worst human being to say it that way. But that's all that happened, like three kisses, and then I tried to be nice about it and say it was a mistake and he made a joke about it and I thought that was it, because he really didn't talk to me at school at all. It was just a kiss. And when David asked me to go to the prom and he was willing to take me as a friend, I was like, 'Great, that would be fun.' But then he took off, so I don't know what I did."

"You didn't do anything. David and I had an argument in the bathroom and he took off because he was angry."

If that makes M.C. feel better, it is hard to tell. She looks up at me, then back down again at the road.

"The next time I kiss someone, it's going to be someone I really like. The way things are going, I'll probably be an octogenarian, but I'd like to feel like it meant something. I know it's just kissing, but still."

M.C. is right. David's house isn't very far away. It would never have occurred to me to walk. I have a suburban mentality: going anywhere farther than my driveway requires getting into a car. I have no sense of actual walking distances. My rented shoes hurt a little, but I think they would have by now anyway.

There are no lights on in David's house.

"He must have gone to bed." Another possibility that hadn't occurred to me. I assumed somehow that he would be up waiting for me. I'm not sure how I expected him to know I would walk over immediately, but going to bed seems almost rude.

"We should wake him up. You guys need to talk."

"I'm not knocking on his door."

"Mitchell, what did you expect to happen once we got here?"

"I don't know. I expected him to be up, watching TV or something."

"Why would he be watching TV?"

It's what I would have done. I would have gone home, turned on the TV to whatever rerun I could find, and spent the rest of the night pretending that none of this had happened. It's really what I want to do now. I start to suggest this to M.C. but she's already walking around to the side of the house.

"Which is his bedroom?"

"The one on the corner. Why?"

"We'll just tap on his window. Thank God for ranch houses. If he was on a second floor, we would have to throw gravel or something."

M.C. has taken over. This is now her project. Why am I such a putz? Of course we could knock on David's window. No more putziness. I am going to be active. I go up to the window. I have to negotiate a rather large and prickly shrub, which is probably staining my tux, but I am now undaunted. I reach over the green impediment to knock on the pane, but there isn't anything there. I flail around a little, but no glass.

"The window's open," I tell M.C.

She starts to giggle. I'm in a white tux standing in a shrub failing to knock on a window. Maybe she has cause.

I lean into the window. "David," I whisper. "David—it's Mitchell. David?"

I look back at M.C. for guidance.

"Is he a sound sleeper?"

"I don't know. I've never seen him sleep."

"Why don't you just climb in?"

Okay. Breaking and entering. I step back to make sure that this is, in fact, the right house, but of course it is. I heave myself over the window ledge and into the room. Easier than it looks. Good thing I'm not a burglar.

"David," I whisper again. I try to remember the layout of his room and walk with my hands outstretched but still crash into his desk chair. He can't be in this room. I follow the wall to the door and run my hands around the frame until I find the light. I flick it on. The room is empty.

The one single-syllable word none of us have used yet

M.C.'s head appears in the window.

"He isn't here," I whisper.

282

"I'm coming in," she tells me, as if maybe he is hiding somewhere and she'll be able to find him. She takes off my tux jacket and throws it inside, then places her hands on the sill and swings one leg over. She manages the window pretty well considering she's dressed in taffeta and heels.

"You're right, he's not here," she declares.

"Now what?"

"We wait. He has to come back."

"Where the hell could he be?"

"At a friend's house?"

"I don't think he has any other friends."

"What about Mariel?"

"She's at somebody's lake house this weekend."

"Maybe he went to one of the after-parties."

"By himself?"

She shrugs. We sit on the bed.

"Maybe we should turn off the light," I suggest. "I don't want his mom to think he's home if he isn't."

She nods and I stand up and turn off the light, then go back and sit beside her on the bed. I don't think about the fact that we are sitting on a bed in a dark room until I'm already sitting down, at which point it feels like it would be more of a statement to stand back up and move to the chair, presuming I could find the chair in the dark. We aren't touching, but I can feel her beside me.

"Mitchell?"

"What?"

"Were you like, you know, sort of—well, in love with Danielle?"

I hadn't thought of it in those terms. Was I in love? It seems like such a big word for one syllable.

"I'm not sure. I was sort of blown away that she even wanted to go out with me. I mean, no one has ever been interested in me at all, and then it was Danielle—well, you know, Danielle was Danielle and I don't know. For a little while I believed."

"Other people have been interested in you. You just never notice."

"Oh, Amanda. I didn't know, I thought she was, but then . . ." I flail around looking for a word and brush M.C.'s bare shoulder. I hadn't realized how close together we were sitting. "Sorry," I say, knowing that I'm blushing but also that she can't see I'm blushing. "I guess maybe I should have asked her out, but I didn't know Amanda really liked me. I thought she was just looking for a prom date."

"I wasn't talking about Amanda. I think she *was* looking for a prom date, mostly."

"Oh."

"I mean, I'm sure she liked you, but she didn't know you very well. But other people have been interested. You're, like, a really nice guy and you're cute and smart, and I'm such an idiot and I can't believe I'm telling you this."

"Telling me what?"

M.C. doesn't respond immediately. I hear her take a deep breath, the kind you take before jumping off the high dive at the pool. "That I would have gone out with you if you had asked, but you wouldn't have asked me because I'm like your sister's dorky friend who's over all the time and in your way and stuff, and I think I need to go home now." She starts to get up. I touch her arm and she sits back down.

I turn toward her. There isn't enough light to really see her face, she is just a dark blotch in a dark room, but I turn toward her anyway. I'm not sure I heard what I think I heard, but I think I know what she said and I think what I want to do right now is kiss her.

My kissing experience is pretty limited, but it seems like there's this moment just before you kiss someone for the first time where there is a question, then you have to wait for a response, for a yes. I'm not sure how you know it's a yes, it isn't a nod or some visible signal, but it's a yes. I don't ask M.C. if it would be okay if I kissed her. For once my natural silence, the quiet non-voice I've been trying to overcome, is the right response. And she no longer seems to be the same M.C. I've always known. She is suddenly someone new—familiar but not the same. It's as if you stepped out of your house and there was this tree in your front yard that you never really noticed before—you knew it was there, but you hadn't really seen it and it's beautiful and green and so obvious that you can't believe you've never stopped and really looked at it, not until right now. Even in the darkness I can picture M.C.'s face perfectly. I know the green eyes, the corners of her mouth, the freckle on her eyelid; all those details are in my head. I know her smile, I know her giggles, I know the look she gets when she's angry, but I never knew I was noticing. I never put it all together. I never wanted to kiss her before. I do now. And, although I can't see her face in this dark room and we bump noses before we touch lips, I know already that her answer is yes.

CHAPTER 31

Regulars

Mostly dressed

David was at my house. I learn this when my father picks me up. Dad is not looking too happy when he pulls into David's driveway. In fact, he's looking a lot like someone who would rather be in bed.

"Maybe you'd better tell me the whole story before we get home. I might be more receptive than your mother."

"It's sort of a long story. It's been sort of a long night."

My dad isn't the heart-to-heart type, and so this is going to be new territory for both of us. I watch him drive and realize that he looks older than I usually think of him as being. His hair is thin. The lines around his eyes are carved deeply. His throat is fleshy, and the pouch of a second chin quivers when he talks, which isn't often. I wonder if he's happy being who he is.

"So," he prompts.

"Where do you want me to begin?"

"How about explaining why I get a call in the middle of the night from David's parents telling me that they found you in David's bed with some girl?"

"We actually weren't doing anything. We were still dressed."

"Mostly dressed, according to David's parents."

"Mostly dressed."

The truth is we had fallen asleep. It felt nice to sleep with my arms around M.C.

At the next stoplight, Dad turns to me. I can tell from his face that he is trying hard to figure out how to handle this situation. "What do you think Amanda's parents would say if they knew?"

"Not much. I wasn't with Amanda."

"That wasn't Amanda?"

"No, Amanda no longer speaks to me. I didn't take her to the prom."

Dad looks confused. David's parents hadn't specified much more than gender before driving the other offending party home, leaving me on the front porch waiting for him. "Weren't you supposed to take Amanda to the prom?"

"Originally, yes, but I took Danielle."

"Oh, right. Well, what do you think Danielle's parents would say?"

"I don't know. She dumped me."

"When did that happen?"

"About 10:30."

The light turns green. "So, who were you in David's bed with?"

"M.C."

"Our M.C.?"

I nod.

"I think maybe you'd better tell me the whole story."

So I tell my father most of the story, except for the part about peeing on my pants and David accusing me of stomping on his heart. With these omissions, the story is a lot shorter and makes almost no sense, but my father appears to be happy that I'm confiding in him at all.

"That would explain why David is sleeping on our couch," Dad tells me as we pull up to our house.

It doesn't, not exactly, but at least I now know where he is.

⊙   ⊙   ⊙

I can't tell whether I wake him up when I come in or whether he was already awake and just lying there with his eyes closed. Either way, when I walk in he opens his eyes. He doesn't look at me, though. He just stares at the ceiling. I'm not sure what to make of that.

"How long have you been here?" I ask.

"Since I left the prom. Where have you been?"

"Your house."

"Why?"

"I was looking for you."

"I was here," David says and sits up. He is dressed in his tuxedo shirt and pants. His hair is matted down on one side and sticking straight up on the other. He reaches over to the coffee table and retrieves his glasses. His face without the glasses looks blank, unfinished. When he puts them on and looks up, he's the David I know. I realize that I had been waiting to gauge his expression. How angry is he?

David smiles. A full smile is a rare event, and it catches me off guard.

"So you were waiting at my house?"

I nod.

"Don't you think that's funny?"

Maybe. "David, there's something else I think you should know."

"Can we get coffee first?"

"Not here. My parents never wash the coffeepot."

"Or vacuum the sofa. Is this thing made of dog hair?"

Not really funny

We go to the Waffle House since it's open all night. It isn't a long drive and we don't talk much on the way. David spends most of the ride trying to get his neck to crack. We are both in our tuxedo remnants, except I changed into a pair of jeans. I may have to bleach the rentals. We look like we could use some coffee.

The Waffle House is always half-full anytime you go.

Two in the afternoon looks a lot like two in the morning. But you haven't had a real Waffle House experience unless you've slid into one of the vinyl booths at about 4 a.m. It is still only about half-full, but at 4 a.m. it is half-full of the hard core. If you're there at that time it is because you have been up all night or because you have some reason to wake up while it is still night. It is truck drivers, club closers, insomniacs, medical residents, and some people who look like they might not have a bed they could go to. There are early risers too, the kind of people who have showered, shaved, and read most of the paper before the coffee arrives. They sit on the stools impatiently waiting for the rest of the world to get it together. We choose a booth near the window, since you never voluntarily take one near the bathroom, and order our hash browns, eggs, bacon, and pancakes. And coffee. We both need coffee.

"Okay. Tell me. What is it that I should know?"

"I wasn't by myself when I went to look for you."

"Couldn't have been Danielle, must have been M.C."

I nod.

"So?"

"Well, we waited for you a long time and we had the light off because we had crawled through the window and we didn't want to wake up your parents and then we were kissing and then . . ."

"You had sex with M.C. in my bed?" Two older guys at the counter turn and look at us. They are up-all-nighters and look a little bleary-eyed, but that caught their attention. The waitress brings our coffee and I wait until she leaves. The counter guys have turned back to their eggs.

"No. We didn't get that far," I whisper. "But your parents found us in your bed and M.C. wasn't completely in her dress anymore and they freaked out a little and then called our parents . . ."

I look up and David is holding his hand under his nose, having some sort of convulsion. "Ouch," he says. "I just snorted coffee out my nose."

"Are you okay?"

"Oh, yeah, I'm fine," he says. Then he breaks down and giggles. David has deep giggles, nearly silent. He finally recovers and asks me, "You don't find any of this funny, do you?"

"Getting caught with M.C. . . . ."

"My prom date."

"Your prom date in your bed by your parents?"

"Not funny?"

"Not funny."

"There's something you should know, too," David says, taking another sip of his coffee and making a face. "Pass the sugar. Thanks. I took your sister home last night."

"You slept with my sister?" I say this a little louder than I meant to and several of the early-morning regulars turn around to look at us. One of the guys at the counter nearly chokes on his toast.

David smiles and gives me his what-an-idiot headshake. "I'm gay, Mitchell."

I will myself not to look around to see the regulars' reaction to that statement.

"I know. But I thought maybe something changed."

"No, I'm still gay."

"Well, that's a relief," I tell him. David actually laughs. Something has changed, and it isn't his sexual orientation.

David takes another sip of his coffee and readjusts his glasses. "When I left the prom, I went and picked up the car. As I pulled out of the parking lot, I almost ran over these two people stumbling down the ramp. I looked up and realized it was Seth and Carrie. Did they even make it into the prom? I don't remember seeing them."

"I was a little preoccupied. I didn't notice."

"Anyway, Seth was so stoned he couldn't stand up and he was leaning heavily on Carrie, who seemed sober but totally pissed off. Well, she had cause. He had puked all over her dress." I grimace. That's pretty gross. It wasn't a great clothing night for the Wells family. "Anyway, she flagged me down and I helped her load Seth into the backseat. Then she looked down at her dress and let loose the longest string of obscenities I have heard someone use in one sentence—male or female. It was something. Usually when someone's mad, they use the same three cuss words over and over. Carrie emptied out the dictionary. Then she looks up at me, smiles, and asks for my tux jacket. Right there in the parking lot, she puts on the tux jacket, buttons it up, and slides off her dress. She's not shy, is she?"

"Never has been."

"Well, she takes the dress, balls it up, and throws it at Seth, calls him a few more names. Then she climbs in the passenger's seat, turns to me sweetly, and asks if I can take her home. So I did. We dropped Seth off on his front porch first—his mother might be a little surprised when she walks out in her bathrobe to fetch the morning paper—and we went home and sat up and talked."

"You and Carrie?"

"Yeah. You didn't tell me she had read my letter."

"Well, it's not like I showed it to her. She went in my desk."

"I know." David pauses while the waitress lays down our food. I realize that I'm actually pretty hungry.

"She called me a chickenshit."

"That sounds like Carrie."

"Yeah, your sister has balls. She thinks that I, um . . . had a thing for you because you're safe. Saved me from having to really deal with my sexuality by focusing on someone who I knew wasn't going to do anything anyway. Keeps it all abstract. Asexual."

I think I'm offended. "How does she know? I could be gay."

"You're not."

"I'm not. Do you think she's right?"

David begins to cut his pancakes. There is a methodology to his pancake slicing, first lengthwise strips and then even crosscuts. Only when they are reduced to little squares does he allow himself a bite. He doesn't look up, but his voice is steady. "I don't know. Maybe. I'm not sure what I want."

"You sound like Danielle."

"She knew what she wanted. Sorry, that's not fair. It sucked what happened last night. I was a sucky friend too. I could have been more . . . something. Supportive. Laughed harder after you pissed on yourself. *Something.*"

"You weren't much help."

"Yeah. I know. So I talked to Carrie and she goes off to bed, not with me, and I go outside and get back in my car. I had decided I was going to go up to find Mariel and hang out at the lake and pretend the prom never happened. But I don't have the address and, as you know, I don't have a cell phone. I almost decide to just drive up there anyway and try to find them, since I know what little town they're in, and it sounds like something you'd be willing to do with me, and only you'd be willing to do with me. I look over at the empty passenger seat and something you said once started going through my mind. I think it was when I was puking in your driveway, but you told me that you needed me to be your friend. You were probably just trying to get me out of your yard, but it didn't feel like nothing. It felt like something I wasn't willing to give up on yet."

David doesn't look up as he says this, but I know he's not talking to his hash browns. When he does look up it's only to shrug and start forking more food into his mouth. We sit silently for a minute or two, then he asks about how I got out of the bathroom and I tell him. "Only Louis could pull that off," he says, shaking his head. He then orders a second round of onion-smothered, cheese-covered hash browns and I drink more coffee. The counter guys are still there when we pay our bill, but most of the late-nighters have moved on and the more normal hardworking early-morning types have taken over.

Not so bad

David seems more relaxed than I have seen him in a long time as we pull out of the Waffle House parking lot.

"What is with you this morning?" I have to ask.

"I don't know. I got to do some thinking last night. You know, we aren't paraplegics."

"Okay."

"And we aren't homeless and our parents don't beat us . . ."

"And we have all of our teeth."

"And we have all of our teeth. We're going to be seniors next year and then go to college." I wait, but this appears to be the end of his soliloquy.

"Okay. So?"

"So," David says, smiling again, "we're not doing so bad."

We ponder this for a while. David pulls into my driveway and I open the car door. I feel like I'm supposed to say something now, but for the life of me I can't think what. David doesn't help, he just looks at me expectantly, like he also thinks I should say something, but I doubt he knows what it is either. All I actually say is, "I'll see you tomorrow," which seems like enough. Statement, not a question. Punctuation matters.

CHAPTER 32

Monday, Again

Curtis returns

And suddenly Curtis is back. We walk into class and there he is. He doesn't explain his absence, doesn't even greet us, although something in his attempt at ruthless normalcy makes me think he is pleased to be back. The desk, moved to the front of the room by Ms. Chimneystack, is back against the side wall, the stool back in front, and he is already lecturing and writing on the board before we even have a chance to sit down.

"I'm assuming that you have at least begun *Portrait of the Artist as a Young Man*, which is easily the most accessible novel Joyce wrote—*Dubliners* doesn't count because it is a collection of short stories and not a novel—but despite the relative ease with which an even moderately attentive reader would comprehend this work, most of you will no doubt complain that it is much too difficult, and it certainly will be if you don't bother to read it. I'd also recommend

Portrait of the Artist as a Young Dog, which is not Joyce but Dylan Thomas, but it has a wonderful title, it's not a bad bit of poetry, and it makes a nice companion piece and a wonderful graduation gift."

Curtis pauses for a moment and looks at me. It looks like he's about to smile, but instead he picks up his monologue at the same rapid pace. "Let's start at the beginning, which is a great place to start for every book, except perhaps *Finnegans Wake*, where the beginning is the predicate of the last sentence, but you haven't read that and, in all likelihood, never will. Would you please get settled, class has begun."

It certainly has. I'm not sure whether he is nervous or has simply stored up several weeks' worth of pompous energy. He talks without pausing for forty-five minutes and then dismisses us with "Please come prepared to discuss the first forty pages tomorrow," which is Curtis code for "Tomorrow we are having a pop quiz." He then turns back to the board to write his notes for the next class.

"Welcome back," Louis grumbles as he leaves. It sounds like sarcasm, but it's honest in its own way.

I had been practicing my "I heard about your mother and I'm glad that she's recovering" line, but I'm not sure I can get it out. Curtis, finished scrawling on the board, turns around and seems to be surprised to find me standing there. He smiles at me and nods. I smile back—at least I think that's what my face is doing. It is, for a moment, like we're talking but we aren't saying anything. He picks up his chalk, like he just thought of something new to write, and I pick up my backpack and move toward the door.

Dr. VandeNeer

The man looks so sincere. White hair, cut short with no signs of a creeping forehead or encroaching baldness, early sixties, large, but he carries his weight well. He exudes warmth and trust. An ordained minister and CEO of a successful day school, Dr. VandeNeer has chosen his vocations well.

With everything that's happened, I'd almost forgotten that I still hadn't had my audience with the headmaster so that he could pass judgment on my crimes. His assistant, who is much more polite than Sorrelson's, casually approached me in the hallway on my way into chemistry to let me know that the doctor had been away and was sorry we didn't get a chance to talk last week, but if I could come to the office during lunch, he would have time to meet with me. Mariel, in a quiet show of sympathy, does the entire lab by herself without my input while I sit on a chair and try to dredge up some emotion at my impending punishment. I am so burnt out from the weekend that I'm not sure I even care what happens to me next.

When I go to the office at lunch, David is waiting for me.

"Why are you here?" I ask.

"I made half of the film," he says.

"But you weren't the one who turned it in as an English project."

"I believe you are in trouble because of the content, not the fact that it was a shitty substitute for a three-to-five-page paper on *The Grapes of Wrath*. I helped with the content."

"You don't have to do this."

"Actually," he says, "I do."

Dr. VandeNeer invites us into his office, three sides of which are covered from floor to ceiling in dark maple bookshelves, filled neatly with books that might have been chosen for the deep, rich colors of their spines, but I suspect that he has actually read most of them. No book jackets, all hardbacks. His desk is just this side of imposing, with enough paper and scattered correspondence to make it acceptably active, a true working space but also spare: solid, oak, no computer, a plain black phone. I check to make sure the phone has buttons, half expecting a rotary dial.

He wears a gray cashmere sweater, no stains, no dog hair, over a pale blue oxford shirt tucked neatly into gray slacks. Unscuffed loafers complete the ensemble. Not a hair out of place, no lunch remnants in his teeth. The one flaw in his appearance is a clearly visible booger hanging from the hairs in his left nostril. This commands my attention for the entirety of the interview. It's hard to concentrate on what he is saying, or at least it would be if what he's saying weren't so shocking.

"Are you here as legal representation or moral support?" he asks David.

"Neither. I helped make the video. Mitchell didn't tell anyone that because he didn't want to get me in trouble. We were supposed to turn it in together, but I chickened out."

Dr. VandeNeer looks at David carefully without speaking. He's not angry and he isn't accusing David of lying, but his eyes are probing for a truth he knows he hasn't heard yet. Then he smiles, as if he now has the answer he was looking for.

"I apologize for not attending to this matter sooner," he tells us in a smooth Southern drawl. "Mr. Sorrelson gave me the DVD last week. I quite enjoyed your cartoon. Is it easy to make copies?"

"You enjoyed our film?" David asks.

"I thought it was hysterical."

"You weren't offended?"

He smiles warmly and his breath comes out in a half chortle. "Was it meant to be offensive?"

God, he's good at this.

"Not to you. Possibly to Steinbeck," I volunteer.

"He's dead, you know. Makes him an easy target." Dr. VandeNeer raises his eyebrows and laughs again, making the booger dance a little, but it hangs on. Sensing my discomfort, he continues, "The Adam and Eve sequence is clearly modeled after Hieronymus Bosch's *The Garden of*

Earthly Delights—quite clever but a mite obscure even for honors English. Not many high-school students are familiar with fourteenth-century medieval painters."

"Bosch is Mr. Wallman's favorite painter," I find myself explaining. I don't mention that he uses that painting as an example in his lecture about sex and violence throughout history.

"I'm sure he was honored that you included it. I see, Mitchell, that Mr. Sorrelson spoke to your parents already and that they expressed support for your project. I believe that your mother called it 'damn creative,' and recommended posting it on the school Web site. I don't believe Mr. Sorrelson followed up on that suggestion. I hope you appreciate that you have great parents."

"They're, yeah, great." This is hard to admit, even to an adult.

"Your mother could be a little kinder toward our baseball umpires, but she has a lot of spirit. I see her often at the games. And I believe your dad was taking care of Mr. Curtis's mother. We are all appreciative of how wonderful he has been during such a difficult time for one of our best teachers."

The man has done his homework.

Dr. VandeNeer picks up the notes from the Judicial Board meeting. "Let's see, the other questionable scenes were: a macabre sewing machine incident—well, that should have pleased the Bible-thumpers. Adam as a sinner is hardly revolutionary, although Christianizing Kafka is an interpretive stretch."

I'm too proud of his assumption that we were interpreting anything to respond.

"And, although the sacrifice of Isaac on a pile of required summer reading is a rather unfair commentary on our English curriculum, it hardly qualifies as blasphemy in this context. It was wise of you to avoid any crucifixion scenes—then you'd be up a creek—but frankly I can't see anything remotely wrong with the cartoon except . . ."

He pauses. I hold my breath. Things are going so well that the "except" catches me by surprise.

"I'd have to disagree with Mr. Curtis's A–. As far as I can tell, with the exception of a rather contrived dust bowl scene, this cartoon has absolutely nothing to do with *The Grapes of Wrath*, certainly no more than it would have if you had turned in a sequence of angry grapes doing ballet. But, as policy, the administration does not interfere with grades, and granting you an A– is well within Mr. Curtis's purview. I am curious, however. Did you actually read the book?"

At least we can both honestly answer yes.

Lunch

"He gave you an A–! I can't believe that."

Rather than being happy that we escaped any serious

disciplinary action, David is just pissed that I made a better grade than he did on the assignment.

"Wallman only gave us a B+ on it."

"Maybe Curtis secretly hates Steinbeck too."

When we enter the lunchroom, M.C. is sitting alone at our table. She scoots her chair over and I sit beside her. David sits opposite us and unpacks his lunch. M.C. steals his apple, but he doesn't complain.

"So what happened?" M.C. asks.

"Nothing."

"Nothing?"

"He liked it. He thought it was funny. He wants us to make him a copy."

M.C. starts to giggle and David actually smiles.

"So that's it?" she asks.

"I guess so."

M.C. takes a bite of her apple, shifts it to her left hand, and reaches down to hold my hand. "I tried to call you yesterday," I tell her. "Your brother said that you were grounded for life."

"Originally they grounded me until I turned twenty-one or entered a convent, whichever came first, but they relented after I calmly and rationally explained the difference between being *on* a bed and *in* a bed, and I swore to them on a stack of Bibles that all the essential parts of my dress were still intact when we were discovered. That and several hours of crying and begging pretty much did the trick. I think that it helped that I was with you. They think you're harmless."

Maybe. Okay, definitely. Safe, harmless. Just what every seventeen-year-old boy wants to be.

"I'm still a little bit grounded. I've almost convinced them to let me ride home from school with you, assuming I wear a chastity belt and am kept under strict supervision, but I can't go out for two weeks. I mean, that's assuming . . ."

"Yes, I would."

M.C. smiles and lays her head on my shoulder.

"Are you in any trouble at all?"

"I don't think so. I think my parents are just happy that I did something normal for teenage boys." My mother's take on the weekend's escapades had been a little out of character. She seemed elated that I was found in bed with my sister's best friend. Maybe she's just relieved it wasn't Danielle. Carrie isn't nearly as thrilled. She hasn't spoken to me at all since she heard. She'll get over it.

There's a short silence. M.C. is thinking. "Were they worried that you were gay?"

I hadn't thought about that. I look across at David, who is watching all of this with a look of slight amusement on his face. "I don't think so. Just pathetic."

David smiles. "It's okay. I already told her. I stopped by her house yesterday."

"He brought me flowers," M.C. says happily.

"I felt badly about leaving her at the prom." I had forgotten that I wasn't the only one who'd been abandoned by a date. Counting Ryan's date and Nicole, there was a lot of dumping going on. I wonder if that happens a lot at proms. "I assume Danielle brought you flowers too?" Still the same smile.

"She has spent the whole day hiding from me. I'll have to talk to her at some point."

"No rush," says M.C.

I look over at David. I know that there's more we have to talk about, but maybe today we can just eat lunch.

"Are you going to eat all of that sandwich?" I ask.

"Yes," he answers. And he does.

ACKNOWLEDGMENTS

For a project this long in the making, I am bound to forget to thank someone, but there are a few people I have to mention. First of all, the original members of my writing group, Laurie Faria Stolarz, Lara Zeises, and Tea Benduhn, not only gave great feedback but also mentored me through this process. They are also all great writers—check out their books. I have also been blessed with a fabulous agent in Rosemary Stimola and amazing editors—Jill Davis, Michelle Nagler, and Caroline Abbey. A special thank you to Bert Harrill and David Brakke for their friendship. Without the encouragement and support from my friends and family (siblings, parents, babysitting in-laws, e-mailing niece), this novel would still be in boxes on the attic floor, so I need to thank you as well. As for Kat, Lev, and Theo—I can't even begin to list all of the ways I'm grateful to have such an incredible family and how lucky I feel when I wake up to another day with you, so I'm just going to say I love you and leave it at that.

STEVEN GOLDMAN lives in Boston, Massachusetts, with his wife and two sons. *Two Parties, One Tux, and a Very Short Film about* The Grapes of Wrath is his first young-adult novel. He has never read *The Grapes of Wrath*.

www.stevengoldmanbooks.com